Horatio Alger

Frank's Campaign

The Farm and the Camp

Horatio Alger

Frank's Campaign
The Farm and the Camp

ISBN/EAN: 9783337814267

Printed in Europe, USA, Canada, Australia, Japan

Cover: Foto ©Thomas Meinert / pixelio.de

More available books at **www.hansebooks.com**

FRANK'S CAMPAIGN;

OR,

THE FARM AND THE CAMP.

BY

HORATIO ALGER, Jr.,

AUTHOR OF "RAGGED DICK SERIES," "LUCK AND PLUCK SERIES."

PHILADELPHIA
PORTER & COATES.

FAMOUS ALGER BOOKS.

Illustrated, Cloth, Extra, Black and Gold.

RAGGED DICK SERIES. Complete in six vols. Price per vol., $1 25.

Ragged Dick; or, Street Life in New York.
Fame and Fortune; or, The Progress of Richard Hunter.
Mark the Match Boy.
Rough and Ready; or, Life among the New York Newsboys.
Ben the Luggage-Boy; or, Among the Wharves.
Rufus and Rose; or, The Fortunes of Rough and Ready.

TATTERED TOM SERIES. A Continuation of the Ragged Dick Series.
Price per vol., $1 25.

First Series.   Complete in four vols.

Tattered Tom; or, The Story of a Street Arab.
Paul the Peddler; or, The Adventures of a Young Street Merchant.
Phil the Fiddler; or, The Young Street Musician.
Slow and Sure; or, From the Sidewalk to the Shop.

Second Series.   Complete in four vols.

Julius; or, The Street Boy out West.
The Young Outlaw; or, Adrift in the World.
Sam's Chance, and How he Improved It.
The District Telegraph Boy.

CAMPAIGN SERIES. Complete in three vols. Price per vol., $1 25.

Frank's Campaign.
Paul Prescott's Charge.
Charlie Codman's Cruise.

LUCK AND PLUCK SERIES. Price per vol., $1 50.

First Series.   Complete in four vols.

Luck and Pluck; or, John Oakley's Inheritance.
Sink or Swim; or, Harry Raymond's Resolve.
Strong and Steady; or, Paddle your Own Canoe.
Strive and Succeed; or, The Progress of Walter Conrad.

Second Series.   Complete in four vols.

Try and Trust; or, The Story of a Bound Boy.
Bound to Rise; or, How Harry Walton Rose in the World.
Risen from the Ranks; or, Harry Walton's Success.
Herbert Carter's Legacy; or, The Inventor's Son.

BRAVE AND BOLD SERIES. Complete in four vols. Price per vol., $1 50.

Brave and Bold; or, The Story of a Factory Boy.
Jack's Ward; or, The Boy Guardian.
Shifting for Himself; or, Gilbert Greyson's Fortunes.
Wait and Hope; or, Ben Bradford's Motto.

PACIFIC SERIES. Complete in four vols. Price per vol., $1 25.

The Young Adventurer; or, Tom's Trip across the Plains.
The Young Miner; or, Tom Nelson in California.
The Young Explorers; or, Among the Sierras.

(Fourth volume in preparation.)

To

CHARLES EDWARD PAINE,

IN MEMORY OF PLEASANT HOURS PASSED TOGETHE

AT NAPLES AND SORRENTO,

This Volume is Inscribed,

BY HIS SINCERE FRIEND

THE AUTHOR.

696715

PREFACE.

"FRANK'S Campaign" is the record of a boy's experiences, by whom the cares and responsibilities of manhood are voluntarily assumed, and nobly and successfully borne. He supplies his father's place while the latter is absent in his country's service, and is enabled, by a fortunate circumstance, to pay off a mortgage resting on the home farm.

Nothing is claimed for the young hero which may not be achieved by an energetic and manly boy of the same age. It is hoped that the record

of Frank's struggles and final success may stimu-
late the boys who may read it to manly endeavor,
and to a faithful and conscientious discharge of
whatever duties may devolve upon them.

CONTENTS.

.

FRANK'S CAMPAIGN;

OR,

THE FARM AND THE CAMP.

I.

THE WAR MEETING.

THE Town Hall in Rossville stands on a moderate elevation overlooking the principal street. It is
generally open only when a meeting has been called
by the Selectmen to transact town business, or occasionally in the evening when a lecture on Temper-
ance or a political address is to be delivered. Rossville is not large enough to sustain a course of
lyceum lectures, and the towns-people are obliged
to depend for intellectual nutriment upon such chance
occasions as these. The majority of the inhabitants
being engaged in agricultural pursuits, the population is somewhat scattered, and the houses, with the
exception of a few grouped around the stores, stand

at respectable distances, each encamped on a farm of
its own.

One Wednesday afternoon, towards the close of
September, 1862, a group of men and boys might
have been seen standing on the steps and in the
entry of the Town House. Why they had met will
best appear from a large placard, which had been
posted up on barns and fences and inside the village
store and post-office.

It ran as follows : —

WAR MEETING!

The citizens of Rossville are invited to meet at the Town
Hall, on Wednesday, September 24, at 3 P. M. to decide what
measures shall be taken towards raising the town's quota of
twenty-five men, under the recent call of the President of the
United States. All patriotic citizens, who are in favor of sus-
taining the free institutions transmitted to us by our fathers,
are urgently invited to be present.

The Hon. Solomon Stoddard is expected to address the meeting.

Come one, come all.

At the appointed hour about one hundred and fifty
men had assembled in the hall. They stood in
groups, discussing the recent call and the general
management of the war with that spirit of independent criticism which so eminently characterizes the
little democracies which make up our New England
States.

" The whole thing has been mismanaged from the

first," remarked a sapient-looking man with a gaunt, cadaverous face, addressing two listeners. "The Administration is corrupt; our generals are either incompetent or purposely inefficient. We haven't got an officer that can hold a candle to General Lee. Abram Lincoln has called for six hundred thousand men. What'll he do with 'em when he gets 'em? Just nothing at all. They'll melt away like snow, and then he'll call for more men. Give me a third of six hundred thousand and I'll walk into Richmond in less 'n thirty days."

A quiet smile played over the face of one of the listeners. With a slight shade of irony in his voice he said, "If such are your convictions, Mr. Holman, I think it a great pity that you are not in the service. We need those who have clear views of what is required in the present emergency. Don't you intend to volunteer?"

"I! " exclaimed the other with lofty scorn. "No sir; I wash my hands of the whole matter. I ain't clear about the justice of warring upon our erring brethren at all. I have no doubt they would be inclined to accept overtures of peace if accompanied with suitable concessions. Still, if war must be waged, I believe I could manage matters infinitely better than Lincoln and his cabinet have done."

"Wouldn't it be well to give them the benefit of your ideas on the subject?" suggested the other quietly.

"Ahem!" said Mr. Holman, a little suspiciously. "What do you mean, Mr. Frost?"

"Only this, that if, like you, I had a definite scheme, which I thought likely to terminate the war, I should feel it my duty to communicate it to the proper authorities, that they might take it into consideration."

"It wouldn't do any good," returned Holman, still a little suspicious that he was quietly laughed at. "They're too set in their own ways to be changed."

At this moment there was a sharp rap on the table, and a voice was heard, saying, "The meeting will please come to order."

The buzz of voices died away, and all eyes were turned towards the speaker's stand.

"It will be necessary to select a chairman to preside over your deliberations," was next heard. "Will any one nominate?"

"I nominate Dr. Plunkett," came from a man in the corner.

The motion was seconded, and a show of hands resulted in favor of the nominee.

A gentlemanly looking man with a pleasant face advanced to the speaker's stand, and with a bow made a few remarks to this effect: —

"Fellow-citizens: this is new business to me, as you are doubtless aware. My professional engagements have not often allowed me to take part in the meetings which from time to time you have held in this hall. On the present occasion, however, I have felt it to be my duty, and the duty of every loyal citizen, to show by his presence how heartily he approves the object which has called us together. The same consideration will not suffer me to decline the unexpected responsibility which you have devolved upon me. Before proceeding further, I would suggest that a clerk will be needed to complete the organization."

A young man was nominated and elected without opposition.

Dr. Plunkett again addressed the meeting: "It is hardly necessary," he said, "to remind you of the object which has brought us together. Our forces in the field need replenishing. The Rebellion has assumed more formidable proportions than we anticipated. It is quite clear that we cannot put it down with one hand. We shall need both. Impressed with this conviction, President Lincoln has made an extraordinary levy upon the country. He feels that it is desirable to put down the Rebellion as speedily as possible, and not suffer it to drag though a series of years. But he cannot work single-handed. The loyal States must give their hearty coöperation. Our State, though inferior in extent and population to some others, has not fallen behind in loyal devotion. Nor, I believe, will Rossville be found wanting in this emergency. Twenty-five men have been

2

called for. How shall we get them? This is the question which we are called upon to consider. I had hoped the Hon. Solomon Stoddard would be here to address you; but I regret to learn that a temporary illness will prevent his doing so. I trust that those present will not be backward in expressing their opinions."

Mr. Holman was already on his feet. His speech consisted of disconnected remarks on the general conduct of the war, mingled with severe denunciation of the Administration.

He had spoken for fifteen minutes in this strain, when the chairman interfered, —

"Your remarks are out of order, Mr. Holman. They are entirely irrelevant to the question."

Holman wiped his cadaverous features with a red silk pocket handkerchief, and inquired, sarcastically, "Am I to understand that freedom of speech is interdicted in this hall?"

"Freedom of speech is in order," said the chairman, calmly, "provided the speaker confines himself to the question under discussion. You have spoken fifteen minutes without once touching it."

"I suppose you want me to praise the Administration," said Holman, evidently thinking that he had demolished the chairman. He looked around to observe what effect his shot had produced.

"That would be equally out of order," ruled the presiding officer. "We have not assembled to

praise or to censure the Administration, but to consider in what manner we shall go to work to raise
our quota."

Holman sat down with the air of a martyr.

Mr. Frost rose next. It is unnecessary to report
his speech. It was plain, practical, and to the point.
He recommended that the town appropriate a certain
sum as bounty money to volunteers. Other towns
had done so, and he thought with good reason. It
would undoubtedly draw in recruits more rapidly.

A short, stout, red-faced man, wearing gold spectacles, rose hastily.

"Mr. Chairman," he commenced, "I oppose that
suggestion. I think it calculated to work serious
mischief. Do our young men need to be hired to
fight for their country? I suppose that is what you
call patriotism. For my part, I trust the town will
have too much good sense to agree to any such
proposition. The consequence of it would be to
plunge us into debt, and increase our taxes to a
formidable amount."

It may be remarked that Squire Haynes, the
speaker, was the wealthiest man in town, and of
course would be considerably affected by increased
taxation. Even now he never paid his annual tax-
bill without an inward groan, feeling that it was so
much deducted from the sum total of his property.

Mr. Frost remained standing while Squire Haynes
was speaking, and at the close continued his speech :

"Squire Haynes objects that my proposition, if adopted, will make our taxes heavier. I grant it : but how can we expect to carry on this gigantic war without personal sacrifices? If they only come in the form of money, we may count ourselves fortunate. I take it for granted that there is not a man here present who does not approve the present war, — who does not feel that we are waging it for good and sufficient reasons."

Here Mr. Holman moved uneasily in his seat, and seemed on the point of interrupting the speaker, but for some reason forebore.

"Such being the case, we cannot but feel that the burden ought to fall upon the entire community, and not wholly upon any particular portion. The heaviest sacrifices must undoubtedly be made by those who leave their homes and peril life and limb on the battle-field. When I propose that you should lighten that sacrifice so far as it lies in your power, by voting them a bounty, it is not because I consider that money will compensate them for the privations they must encounter and the perils they will incur. For that, they must look to the satisfaction that will arise from the feeling that they have responded to their country's call, and done something to save from ruin the institutions which our fathers transmitted as a sacred trust to their descendants. Money cannot pay for loss of life or limb. But some of them leave families behind. It is not right that these families should suffer because the fathers have devoted themselves to the sacred cause of liberty. When our soldiers go forth, enable them to feel that their wives and children shall not lack for the necessaries of life. The least that those who are privileged to stay at home can do is to tax their purses for this end."

"Mr. Chairman," said Squire Haynes, sarcastically, "I infer that the last speaker is intending to enlist."

Mr. Frost's face flushed at this insinuation.

"Squire Haynes chooses to impute to me interested motives. I need enter into no defence before an audience to whom I am well known. I will only inquire whether interested motives have nothing to do with his opposition to voting bounties to our soldiers?"

This was such a palpable hit that Squire Haynes winced under it, and his red face turned redder as he saw the smiles of those about him.

"Impudent puppy!" he muttered to himself; "he seems to forget that I have a mortgage of eight hundred dollars on his farm. When the time comes to foreclose it, I will show him no mercy. I'll sell him up, root and branch!"

Mr. Frost could not read the thoughts that were passing through the mind of his creditor. They might have given him a feeling of uneasiness, but would not in the least have influenced his action. He was a man loyal to his own convictions of duty, and no apprehension of personal loss would have

2*

prevented his speaking in accordance with what he felt to be right.

The considerations which had been urged were so reasonable, that the voters present, with very little opposition, voted to pay one hundred and fifty dollars to each one who was willing to enlist as one of the town's quota. A list was at once opened, and after the close of the meeting four young men came forward and put down their names, amid the applause of the assembly.

"I wanted to do it before," said John Drake, one of the number, to Mr. Frost, "but I've got a wife and two little children dependent upon me for support. I couldn't possibly support them out of my thirteen dollars a month, even with the State aid. But your motion has decided me. I could do better by staying at home, even with that; but that isn't the question. I want to help my country in this hour of her need; and now that my mind is at ease about my family, I shall cheerfully enter the service."

"And I know of no one who will make a **better soldier!**" said Mr. Frost, heartily.

II.

THE PRIZE.

A few rods distant from the Town Hall, but on the opposite side of the street, stood the Rossville Academy. It had been for some years under the charge of James Rathburn, A. M., a thorough scholar and a skilful teacher. A large part of his success was due to his ability in making the ordinary lessons of the schoolroom interesting to his scholars.

Some forty students attended the Academy, mostly from the town of Rossville. Mr. Rathburn, however, received a few boarders into his family.

There were three classes in the Latin language; but the majority of those who had taken it up stopped short before they had gone beyond the Latin Reader. One class, however, had commenced reading the Æneid of Virgil, and was intending to pursue the full course of preparation for college; though in regard to one member of the class there was some doubt whether he would be able to enter college. As this boy is to be our hero we will take a closer look at him.

Frank Frost is at this time in his sixteenth year. He is about the medium size, compactly made, and the healthful color in his cheeks is good evidence that he is not pursuing his studies at the expense of his health. He has dark chestnut hair, with a slight wave, and is altogether a fine-looking boy.

At a desk behind him sits John Haynes, the son of Squire Haynes, introduced in our last chapter. He is nearly two years older than Frank, and about as opposite to him in personal appearance as can well be imagined. He has a thin face, very black hair, is tall of his age, and already beginning to feel himself a young man. His manner is full of pretension. He never forgets that his father is the richest man in town, and can afford to give him advantages superior to those possessed by his school-fellows. He has a moderate share of ability, but is disinclined to work hard. His affectation of superiority makes him as unpopular among his school-fellows as Frank is popular.

These two boys, together with Henry Tufts, constitute the preparatory class of Rossville Academy. Henry is mild in his manners, and a respectable student, but possesses no positive character. He comes from a town ten miles distant, and boards with the Principal. Frank, though the youngest of the three, excels the other two in scholarship. But there is some doubt whether he will be able to go to college. His father is in moderate circumstances, deriving a comfortable subsistence from a small farm, but is able to lay by a very small surplus every year, and this he feels it necessary to hold in reserve for the liquidation of the mortgage held by Squire Haynes. Frank's chance of attaining what he covets — a college education — seems small; but he is resolved at least to prepare for college, feeling that even this will constitute a very respectable education.

The reader is introduced to the main schoolroom of the Rossville Academy on the morning of the day on which the war meeting takes place.

At nine o'clock the bell rang, and the scholars took their seats. After the preliminary devotional exercise, Mr. Rathburn, instead of calling up the first class at once, paused a moment, and spoke as follows : —

" Scholars, I need not remind you that on the first day of the term, with the design of encouraging you to aim at improvement in English composition, I offered two prizes, — one for the best essay written by a boy over fourteen years of age; the other for the best composition by any one under that age. It gives me pleasure to state that in most of those submitted to me I recognize merit, and I should be glad if it were in my power to give three times as many prizes. Those of you, however, who are unsuccessful will feel repaid by the benefit you have yourselves derived from the efforts you have made for another end."

During this address, John Haynes looked about him with an air of complacency and importance.

He felt little doubt that his own essay on the
" Military Genius of Napoleon" would win the
prize. He did not so much care for this, except
for the credit it would give him. But his father,
who was ambitious for him, had promised him twenty-five dollars if he succeeded, and he had already
appropriated this sum in imagination. He had determined to invest it in a handsome boat which he
had seen for sale in Boston on his last visit to that
city.

" After careful consideration," continued the
teacher, " I have decided that the prize should
be adjudged to an essay entitled, ' The Duties of
Boys in the present National Crisis,' written by
Frank Frost."

There was a general clapping of hands at this
announcement. Frank was a general favorite, and
even his disappointed rivals felt a degree of satisfaction in feeling that he had obtained the prize.

There was one exception, however. John Haynes
turned pale, and then red, with anger and vexation.
He scowled darkly while the rest of the boys were
applauding, and persuaded himself that he was the
victim of a great piece of injustice.

Frank's face flushed with pleasure, and his eyes
danced with delight. He had made a great effort to
succeed, and he knew that at home they would be
very happy to hear that the prize had been awarded
to him.

"Frank Frost will come forward," said Mr. Rathburn.

Frank left his seat, and advanced modestly. Mr. Rathburn placed in his hand a neat edition of Whittier's Poems in blue and gold.

"Let this serve as an incentive to renewed effort," he said.

The second prize was awarded to one of the girls. As she has no part in our story, we need say nothing more on this point.

At recess, Frank's desk was surrounded by his schoolmates, who were desirous of examining the prize volumes. All expressed hearty good will, congratulating him on his success, with the exception of John Haynes.

"You seem mighty proud of your books, Frank Frost," said he with a sneer. "We all know that you're old Rathburn's favorite. It didn't make much difference what you wrote, as long as you were sure of the prize."

"For shame, John Haynes!" exclaimed little Harvey Grover, impetuously. "You only say that because you wanted the prize yourself, and you're disappointed."

"Disappointed!" retorted John, scornfully. "I don't want any of old Rathburn's sixpenny books. I can buy as many as I please. If he'd given 'em to me, I should have asked him to keep' em for those who needed 'em more."

Frank was justly indignant at the unfriendly course which John chose to pursue, but feeling that it proceeded from disappointed rivalry, he wisely said nothing to increase his exasperation. He put the two books carefully away in his desk, and settled himself quietly to his day's lessons.

It was not until evening that John and his father met. Both had been chafed, — the first by his disappointment, the second by the failure of his effort to prevent the town's voting bounties to volunteers. In particular he was incensed with Mr. Frost, for his imputation of interested motives, although it was only in return for a similar imputation brought against himself.

"Well, father, I did n't get the prize," commenced John, in a discontented voice.

"So much the worse for you," said his father, coldly. "You might have gained it if you had made an effort."

"No, I could n't. Rathburn was sure to give it to his favorite."

"And who is his favorite?" questioned Squire Haynes, not yet siding with his son.

"Frank Frost, to be sure."

"Frank Frost!" repeated the Squire, rapidly wheeling round to his son's view of the matter. His dislike of the father was so great that it readily included the son. "What makes you think he is the teacher's favorite?"

"O, Rathburn is always praising him for something or other. All the boys know Frank Frost is his pet. You wont catch him praising me, if I work ever so hard."

John did not choose to mention that he had not yet tried this method of securing the teacher's approval.

"Teachers should never have favorites," said the Squire, dogmatically. "It is highly detrimental to a teacher's influence, and subversive of the principles of justice. Have you got your essay with you, John?"

"Yes, sir."

"You may sit down and read it to me, and if I think it deserving, I will take care that you shan't lose by the teacher's injustice."

John readily obeyed. He hurried up to his chamber, and opening his writing-desk took out a sheet of foolscap, three sides of which were written over. This he brought down stairs with him. He began to hope that he might get the boat after all.

The Squire, in dressing-gown and slippers, sat in a comfortable arm-chair, while John in a consequential manner read his rejected essay. It was superficial and commonplace, and abundantly marked with pretension, but to the Squire's warped judgment it seemed to have remarkable merit.

"It does you great credit, John," said he emphatically. "I don't know what sort of an essay young

3

Frost wrote, but I venture to say it was not as good. If he's anything like his father, he is an impertinent jackanapes."

John pricked up his ears, and listened attentively.

"He grossly insulted me at the town-meeting to-day, and I shan't soon forget it. It isn't for his interest to insult a man who has the power to annoy him that I possess."

"Haven't you got a mortgage on his farm?"

"Yes, and at a proper time I shall remind him of it. But to come back to your own affairs. What was the prize given to young Frost?"

"A blue and gold copy of Whittier's Poems, in two volumes."

"Plain binding, I suppose."

"Yes, sir."

"Very well. The next time I go to Boston, I will buy you the same thing bound in calf. I don't intend that you shall suffer by your teacher's injustice."

"It wasn't so much the prize that I cared for," said John, who felt like making the most of his father's favorable mood, "but you know you promised me twenty-five dollars if I gained it."

"And as you have been defrauded of it, I will give you thirty instead," said the Squire, promptly.

John's eyes sparkled with delight. "O, thank you, sir!" he said. "I wouldn't change places with Frank Frost now for all his prize."

"I should think not, indeed," said the Squire, pompously. "Your position as the son of a poor farmer would n't be quite so high as it is now."

As he spoke he glanced complacently at the handsome furniture which surrounded him, the choice engravings which hung on the walls, and the full-length mirror in which his figure was reflected. "Ten years from now Frank Frost will be only a common laborer on his father's farm,—that is," he added significantly, "if his father manages to keep it; while you, I hope, will be winning distinction at the bar."

Father and son were in a congenial mood that evening, and a common hatred drew them more closely together than mutual affection had ever done. They were very much alike, — both cold, calculating, and selfish. The Squire was indeed ambitious for his son, but could hardly be said to love him, since he was incapable of feeling a hearty love for any one except himself.

As for John, it is to be feared that he regarded his father chiefly as one from whom he might expect future favors. His mother had been a good, though not a strong-minded woman, and her influence might have been of advantage to her son; but unhappily she had died when John was in his tenth year, and since then he had become too much like his father.

III.

Mr. Frost's farm was situated about three quarter's of a mile from the village. It comprised fifty acres, of which twenty were suitable for tillage, the remainder being about equally divided between woodland and pasture.

Mr. Frost had for some years before his marriage been a painter, and had managed to save up from his earnings not far from a thousand dollars. Thinking, however, that farming would be more favorable to health, he purchased his fifty acre farm for twenty-eight hundred dollars, payable one thousand down, and the rest remaining on mortgage. At the date of our story he had succeeded in paying up the entire amount within eight hundred dollars, a mortgage for that amount being held by Squire Haynes. He had not been able to accomplish this without strict economy, in which his wife had cheerfully aided him.

But his family had grown larger and more expensive. Besides Frank, who was the oldest, there were now three younger children, — Alice, twelve years of age; Maggie, ten; and Charlie, seven.

The farmhouse was small but comfortable, and

the family had never been tempted to sigh for a more costly or luxurious home. They were happy and contented, and this made their home attractive. .

On the evening succeeding that of the war meeting, Frank was seated in the common sitting-room with his father and mother. There was a well-worn carpet on the floor, a few plain chairs were scattered about the room, and in the corner ticked one of the old-fashioned clocks such as used to be the pride of our New England households. In the centre of the room stood a round table, on which had been set a large kerosene lamp, which diffused a cheerful light about the apartment.

On a little table, over which hung a small mirror, were several papers and magazines. Economical in most things, Mr. Frost was considered by many of his neighbors extravagant in this. He subscribed regularly for *Harper's Magazine* and *Weekly*, a weekly agricultural paper, a daily paper, and a child's magazine.

" I don't see how you can afford to buy so much reading matter," said a neighbor, one day. " It must cost you a sight of money. As for me, I only take a weekly paper, and I think I shall have to give that up soon."

" All my papers and magazines cost me in a year, including postage, is less than twenty dollars," said Mr. Frost, quietly. " A very slight additional economy in dress, — say three dollars a year to each of

us, — will pay that. I think my wife would rather
make her bonnet wear doubly as long than give up a
single one of our papers. When you think of the
comparative amount of pleasure given by a paper
that comes to you fifty-two times in a year, and a
little extra extravagance in dress, I think you will
decide in favor of the paper."

· " But when you 've read it, you have n't anything
to show for your money."

" And when clothes are worn out you may say
the same of them. But we value both for the good
they have done, and the pleasure they have afforded.
I have always observed that a family where papers
and magazines are taken is much more intelligent
and well-informed than where their bodies are clothed
at the expense of their minds. Our daily paper is
the heaviest item ; but I like to know what is passing in the world, and, besides, I think I more than
defray the expense by the knowledge I obtain of the
markets. At what price did you sell your apples
last year ? "

" At one dollar and seventy-five cents per barrel."

" And I sold forty barrels at two dollars per barrel. I found from my paper that there was reason
to expect an increase in the price, and held on. By
so doing I gained ten dollars, which more than paid
the expense of my paper for the year. So even in
a money way I was paid for my subscription. No,
neighbor, though I have good reason to economize,

I don't care to economize in that direction. I want my children to grow up intelligent citizens. Let me advise you, instead of stopping your only paper, to subscribe for two or three more."

" I don't know," was the irresolute reply. " It was pretty lucky about the apples ; but it seems a good deal to pay. As for my children, they don't get much time to read. They've got to earn their livin', and that ain't done by settin' down and readin'."

" I am not so sure of that," said Mr. Frost. " Education often enables a man to make money."

The reader may have been surprised at the ease with which Mr. Frost expressed himself in his speech at the war meeting. No other explanation is required than that he was in the habit of reading, every day, well-selected newspapers. " A man is known by the company he keeps."

" So you gained the prize, Frank?" said his father, approvingly. " I am very glad to hear it. It does you great credit. I hope none were envious of your success."

" Most of the boys seemed glad of it," was the reply ; " but John Haynes was angry because he did n't get it himself. He declared that I succeeded only because I was a favorite with Mr. Rathburn."

" I am afraid he has not an amiable disposition. However, we must remember that his home influences have n't been the best. His mother's death was unfortunate for him."

"I heard at the store that you and Squire Haynes had a discussion at the war meeting," said Frank, inquiringly. "How was it, father?"

"It was on the question of voting a bounty to our volunteers. I felt that such a course would be only just. The Squire objected on the ground that our taxes would be considerably increased."

"And how did the town vote?"

"They sustained my proposition, much to the Squire's indignation. He does n't seem to feel that any sacrifices ought to be expected of him."

"What is the prospect of obtaining the men, father?"

"Four have already enlisted, but twenty-one are still required. I fear there will be some difficulty in obtaining the full number. In a farming town like ours the young men are apt to go off to other places as soon as they are old enough; so that the lot must fall upon some who have families."

Frank sat for some minutes gazing thoughtfully into the wood fire that crackled in the fireplace.

"I wish I was old enough to go, father," he said, at length.

"I wish you were," said his father, earnestly. "Not that it would n't be hard to send you out into the midst of perils; but our duty to our country ought to be paramount to our personal preferences."

"There's another reason," he said, after a while, "why I wish you were older. You could take my place on the farm, and leave me free to enlist. I should have no hesitation in going. I have not forgotten that my grandfather fought at Bunker Hill."

"I know, father," said Frank, nodding; "and that's his musket that hangs up in your room, is n't it?"

"Yes; it was his faithful companion for three years. I often think with pride of his services. I have been trying to think all day whether I could n't make some arrangement to have the farm carried on in my absence; but it is very hard to obtain a person in whom I could confide."

"If I were as good a manager as some," said Mrs. Frost, with a smile, "I would offer to be your farmer; but I am afraid that; though my intentions would be of the best, things would go on badly under my administration."

"You have enough to do in the house, Mary," said her husband. I should not wish you to undertake the additional responsibility, even if you were thoroughly competent. I am afraid I shall have to give up the idea of going."

Mr. Frost took up the evening paper. Frank continued to look thoughtfully into the fire, as if revolving something in his mind. Finally he rose, and lighting a candle went up to bed. But he did not go to sleep for some time. A plan had occurred to him, and he was considering its feasibility.

"I think I could do it," he said, at last, turning over and composing himself to sleep. "I'll speak to father the first thing to-morrow morning."

IV.

FRANK MAKES A PROPOSITION.

WHEN Frank woke the next morning the sun was shining into his window. He rubbed his eyes and tried to think what it was that had occupied his mind the night before. It came to him in a moment, and jumping out of bed he dressed himself with unusual expedition.

Hurrying down stairs, he found his mother in the kitchen, busily engaged in getting breakfast.

" Where's father ? " he asked.

" He has n't come in from the barn yet, Frank," his mother answered. " You can have your breakfast now, if you are in a hurry to get to studying."

" Never mind, just now, mother," returned Frank. " I want to speak to father about something."

Taking his cap from the nail in the entry where it usually hung, Frank went out to the barn. He found that his father was nearly through milking.

" Is breakfast ready ? " asked Mr. Frost, looking up. " Tell your mother she need n't wait for me."

" It is n't ready yet," said Frank. " I came out because I want to speak to you about something very particular."

" Very well, Frank. Go on."

"But if you don't think it a good plan, or think that I am foolish in speaking of it, don't say anything to anybody."

Mr. Frost looked at Frank in some little curiosity.

"Perhaps," he said, smiling, "like our neighbor Holman, you have formed a plan for bringing the war to a close."

Frank laughed. "I am not quite so presumptuous," he said. "You remember saying last night, that if I were old enough to take charge of the farm, you would have no hesitation in volunteering?"

"Yes."

"Don't you think *I am* old enough?" asked Frank, eagerly.

"Why you are only fifteen, Frank," returned his father, in surprise.

"I know it, but I am strong enough to do considerable work."

"It isn't so much that which is required. A man could easily be found to do the hardest of the work. But somebody is needed who understands farming, and is qualified to give directions. How much do you know of that?"

"Not much at present," answered Frank, modestly, "but I think I could learn easily. Besides, there's Mr. Maynard, who is a good farmer, could advise me whenever I was in doubt, and you could write home directions in your letters."

"That is true," said Mr. Frost, thoughtfully.

"I will promise to give it careful consideration. But have you thought that you will be obliged to give up attending school."

"Yes, father."

"And of course that will put you back; your classmates will get in advance of you."

"I have thought of that, father, and I shall be very sorry for it. But I think that is one reason why I desire the plan."

"I don't understand you, Frank," said his father, a little puzzled.

"You see, father, it would require a sacrifice on my part, and I should feel glad to think I had an opportunity of making a sacrifice for the sake of my country."

"That's the right spirit, Frank," said his father, approvingly. "That's the way my grandfather felt and acted, and it's the way I like to see my son feel. So it would be a great sacrifice to me to leave you all."

"And to us to be parted from you, father," said Frank.

"I have no doubt of it, my dear boy," said his father, kindly. "We have always been a happy and united family, and, please God, we always shall be. But this plan of yours requires consideration. I will talk it over with your mother and Mr. Maynard, and will then come to a decision."

"I was afraid you would laugh at me," said Frank.

"No," said his father, "it was a noble thought, and does you credit. I shall feel that, whatever course I may think it wisest to adopt."

The sound of a bell from the house reached them. This meant breakfast. Mr. Frost had finished milking, and with a well-filled pail in either hand, went towards the house.

"Move the milking-stool, Frank," he said, looking behind him, "or the cow will kick it over."

Five minutes later they were at breakfast.

"I have some news for you, Mary," said Mr. Frost, as he helped his wife to a sausage.

"Indeed?" said she, looking up, inquiringly.

"Some one has offered to take charge of the farm for me, in case I wish to go out as a soldier."

"Who is it?" asked Mrs. Frost, with strong interest.

"A gentleman with whom you are well — I may say intimately acquainted," was the smiling response.

"It isn't Mr. Maynard?"

"No. It is some one that lives nearer than he."

"How can that be? He is our nearest neighbor."

"Then you can't guess?"

"No. I am quite mystified."

"Suppose I should say that it is your oldest son?"

"What, Frank?" exclaimed Mrs. Frost, turning from her husband to her son, whose flushed face indicated how anxious he was about his mother's favorable opinion.

4

"You have hit it."

"You were not in earnest, Frank?" said Mrs. Frost, inquiringly.

"Ask father."

"I think he was. He certainly appeared to be."

"But what does Frank know about farming?"

"I asked him that question, myself. He admitted that he didn't know much at present, but thought that, with Mr. Maynard's advice, he might get along."

Mrs. Frost was silent a moment. "It will be a great undertaking," she said, at last; "but if you think you can trust Frank, I will do all I can to help him. I can't bear to think of having you go, yet I am conscious that this is a feeling which I have no right to indulge at the expense of my country."

"Yes," said her husband, seriously. "I feel that I owe my country a service which I have no right to delegate to another, as long as I am able to discharge it myself. I shall reflect seriously upon Frank's proposition."

There was no more said at this time. Both Frank and his parents felt that it was a serious matter, and not to be hastily decided.

After breakfast Frank went up stairs, and before studying his latin lesson, read over thoughtfully the following passage in his prize essay on "The Duties of American Boys at the Present Crisis."

"Now that so large a number of our citizens have

been withdrawn from their families and their ordinary business to engage in putting down this wicked Rebellion, it becomes the duty of the boys to take their places as far as they are able to do so. A boy cannot wholly supply the place of a man, but he can do so in part. And where he is not called on to do this, he can so conduct himself that his friends who are absent may feel at ease about him. He ought to feel willing to give up some pleasures, if by so doing he can help to supply the places of those who are gone. If he does this voluntarily, and in the right spirit, he is just as patriotic as if he were a soldier in the field."

"I did n't think," thought Frank, "when I wrote this, how soon my words would come back to me. It is n't much to write the words. The thing is to stand by them. If father should decide to go, I will do my best, and then, when the Rebellion is over, I shall feel that I did something, even if it was n't much, towards putting it down."

Frank put his essay carefully away in a bureau-drawer in which he kept his clothes, and, spreading open his Latin lexicon, proceeded to prepare his lesson in the third book of Virgil's Æneid.

V.

FRANK'S seat in the schoolroom was directly in front of that occupied by John Haynes. Until the announcement of the prize John and he had been on friendly terms. They belonged to the same class in Latin, and Frank had often helped his classmate through a difficult passage which he had not the patience to construe for himself. Now, however, a coolness grew up between them, originating with John. He felt envious of Frank's success; and this feeling brought with it a certain bitterness which found gratification in anything which he had reason to suppose would annoy Frank.

On the morning succeeding the distribution of the prizes, Frank arrived at the schoolhouse a few minutes before the bell rang. John, with half a dozen other boys, stood near the door.

John took off his hat with mock deference. "Make way for the great prize essayist, gentlemen!" he said. "The modern Macaulay is approaching."

Frank colored with annoyance. John did not fail to notice this with pleasure. He was sorry,

however, that none of the other boys seemed inclined to join in the demonstration. In fact, they
liked Frank much the better of the two.

"That is n't quite fair, John," said Frank, in a
low voice.

"I am always glad to pay my homage to distin-
guished talent," John proceeded, in the same tone.
"I feel how presumptuous I was in venturing to
compete with a gentleman of such genius!"

"Do you mean to insult me?" asked Frank,
growing angry.

"O dear, no! I am only expressing my high
opinion of your talents!"

"Let him alone, John!" said Dick Jones. "It
is n't his fault that the teacher awarded the prize to
him instead of you."

"I hope you don't think I care for that!" said
John, snapping his fingers. "He's welcome to his
rubbishing books; they don't amount to much, any
way. I don't believe they cost more than two dollars at the most. If you 'd like to see what I got
for my essay, I 'll show you."

John pulled out his port-monnaie, and unrolled
three new and crisp bank-notes of ten dollars each.

"I think that 's pretty good pay," he said, looking about him triumphantly. "I don't care how
many prizes Rathburn chooses to give his favorite.
I rather think I can get along without them."

John's face was turned towards the door, other-

4*

wise he would have observed the approach of the
teacher, and spoken with more caution. But it was
too late. The words had been spoken above his
ordinary voice, and were distinctly heard by the
teacher. He looked sharply at John Haynes, whose
glance fell before his, but without a word passed into
the schoolroom.

"See if you don't get a blowing-up, John?"
said Dick Jones.

"What do I care!" said John, but in a tone too
subdued to be heard by any one else. "It won't
do Rathburn any harm to hear the truth for once in
his life."

"Well, I'm glad I'm not in your place, that's
all!" replied Dick.

"You're easily frightened!" rejoined John, with
a sneer.

Nevertheless, as he entered the schoolroom, and
walked with assumed bravado to his seat in the back
part of the room, he did not feel quite so comfortable as he strove to appear. As he glanced stealth-
ily at the face of the teacher, who looked unusually
stern and grave, he could not help thinking, "I
wonder whether he will say anything about it."

Mr. Rathburn commenced in the usual manner;
but after the devotional exercises were over, he
paused, and, after a brief silence, during which
those who had heard John's words listened with
earnest attention, spoke as follows : —

" As I approached the schoolroom this morning I chanced to catch some words which I presume were not intended for my ear. If I remember rightly they were, ' I don't care how many prizes Rathburn gives his favorite ! ' There were several that heard them, so that I can be easily corrected if I have made any mistake. Now I will not affect to misunderstand the charge conveyed by these words. I am accused of assigning the prizes, or at least one of them, yesterday, not with strict regard to the merit of the essays presented, but under the influence of partiality. If this is the real feeling of the speaker, I can only say that I am sorry he should have so low an opinion of me. I do not believe the scholars generally entertain any such suspicion. Though I may err in judgment, I think that most of you will not charge me with anything more serious. If you ask me whether a teacher has favorites, I say that he cannot help having them. He cannot help making a difference between the studious on the one hand, and the indolent and neglectful on the other. But in a matter like this I ask you to believe me when I say that no consideration except that of merit is permitted to weigh. The boy who made this charge is one of my most advanced scholars, and has no reason to believe that he would be treated with unfairness. I do not choose to say any more on this subject, except that I have decided to offer two similar prizes for the two best compositions sub-

mitted within the next four weeks. I shall assign
them to the best of my judgment, without regard to
the scholarship of the writer."

Mr. Rathburn spoke in a quiet, dignified manner,
which convinced all who heard him of his fairness.
I say all, because even John Haynes was persuaded
against his own will, though he did not choose to
acknowledge it. He had a dogged obstinacy which
would not allow him to retract what he had once
said. There was an unpleasant sneer on his face
while the teacher was speaking, which he did not
attempt to conceal.

" The class in Virgil," called Mr. Rathburn.

This class consisted of Frank Frost, John Haynes,
and Henry Tufts. John rose slowly from his seat,
and advanced to the usual place, taking care to stand
as far from Frank as possible.

" You may commence, John," said the teacher.

It was unfortunate for John that he had been
occupied, first, by thoughts of his rejected essay,
and afterwards by thoughts of the boat which he
proposed to buy with the thirty dollars of which he
had become possessed, so that he had found very little time to devote to his Latin. Had he been on
good terms with Frank, he would have asked him to
read over the lesson, which, as he was naturally
quick, would have enabled him to get off passably.
But, of course, under the circumstances, this was
not to be thought of. So he stumbled through two

or three sentences, in an embarrassed manner. Mr.
Rathburn at first helped him along. Finding, however, that he knew little or nothing of the lesson, he
quietly requested Frank to read, saying, "You don't
seem so well prepared as usual, John."

Frank translated fluently and well, his recitation
forming a very favorable contrast to the slipshod attempt of John. This John, in a spirit of unreason-
ableness, magnified into a grave offence, and a desire
to "show off" at his expense.

"Trying to shine at my expense," he muttered.
Well, let him! Two or three years hence, when I
am in college, perhaps things may be a little different."

Frank noticed his repellant look, and it made him
feel uncomfortable. He was a warmhearted boy,
and wanted to be on good terms with everybody.
Still, he could not help feeling that in the present instance he had nothing to reproach himself with.

John went back to his seat feeling an increased
irritation against Frank. He could not help seeing
that he was more popular with his schoolmates than
himself, and of course this too he considered a just
cause of offence against him.

While he was considering in what way he could
slight Frank, the thought of the boat he was about
to purchase entered his mind. He brightened up at
once, for this suggested something. He knew how
much boys like going out upon the water. At pres-

ent there was no boat on the pond.   His would hold
six or eight boys readily.   He would invite some of
the oldest boys to accompany him on his first trip,
carefully omitting Frank Frost.   The slight would
be still more pointed because Frank was his classmate.

When the bell rang for recess he lost no time in
carrying out the scheme he had thought of.

" Dick, " he called out to Dick Jones, " I am
expecting my boat up from Boston next Tuesday,
and I mean to go out in her Wednesday afternoon.
Would n't you like to go with me ? "

" With all the pleasure in life," said Dick, " and
thank you for the invitation."

" How many will she hold ? "

" Eight or ten, I expect.   Bob Ingalls, would you
like to go too ! "

The invitation was eagerly accepted.   John next
approached Henry Tufts, who was speaking with
Frank Frost.

Without even looking at the latter, he asked
Henry if he would like to go.

" Very much," was the reply.

" Then I will expect you, " he said.   He turned
on his heel and walked off without taking any notice
of Frank.

Frank blushed, in spite of himself.

" Don't he mean to invite you ? " asked Henry, in
surprise.

" It appears not," said Frank.

" It's mean in him, then," exclaimed Henry ; " I declare, I 've a great mind not to go."

" I hope you will go," said Frank, hastily. "You will enjoy it. Promise me you will go."

" Would you really prefer to have me ? "

" I should be very sorry if you did n't."

" Then I 'll go ; but I think he 's mean in not asking you, for all that."

VI.

MR. FROST MAKES UP HIS MIND.

"WELL, Frank," said his father at supper-time, "I've been speaking to Mr. Maynard this afternoon about your plan."

"What did he say?" asked Frank, dropping his knife and fork in his eagerness.

"After he had thought a little, he spoke of it favorably. He said that, being too old to go himself, he should be glad to do anything in his power to facilitate my going, if I thought it my duty to do so."

"Didn't he think Frank rather young for such an undertaking?" asked Mrs. Frost, doubtfully.

"Yes, he did; but still, he thought with proper advice and competent assistance he might get along. For the first, he can depend upon Mr. Maynard and myself; as for the second, Mr. Maynard suggested a good man, who is seeking a situation as farm laborer."

"Is it anybody in this town?" asked Frank.

"No, it is a man from Brandon, named Jacob Carter. Mr. Maynard says he is honest, industrious, and used to working on a farm. I shall write to him this evening."

" Then you have decided to go ! " exclaimed Frank and his mother in concert.

" It will depend in part upon the answer I receive from this man, Carter. I shall feel, if he agrees to come, that I can go with less anxiety."

" How we shall miss you ! " said his wife, in a subdued tone.

" And I shall miss you quite as much. It will be a considerable sacrifice for all of us. But when my country has need of me, you will feel that I cannot honorably stay at home. As for · Frank, he may regard me as his substitute."

" My substitute ! " repeated Frank, in a questioning tone.

" Yes, since but for you, taking charge of the farm, in my absence, I should not feel that I could go."

Frank looked pleased. It made him feel that he was really of some importance. Boys, unless they are incorrigibly idle, are glad to be placed in posts of responsibility. Frank, though very modest, felt within himself unused powers and undeveloped capacities, which he knew must be called out by the unusual circumstances in which he would be placed. The thought too that he would be serving his country, even at home, filled him with satisfaction.

After a pause, Mr. Frost said : " There is one point on which I still have some doubts. As you are all equally interested with myself, I think it proper to ask your opinion, and shall abide by your decision."

Frank and his mother listened with earnest attention.

"You are aware that the town has decided to give a bounty of one hundred and fifty dollars to such as may volunteer towards filling the quota. You may remember, also, that although the town passed the vote almost unanimously, it was my proposition, and supported by a speech of mine."

"Squire Haynes opposed it, I think you said, father."

"Yes, and intimated that I urged the matter from interested motives. He said he presumed I intended to enlist."

"As if that sum would pay a man for leaving his home, and incurring the terrible risks of war!" exclaimed Mrs. Frost, looking indignant.

"Very likely he did not believe it himself; but he was irritated with me, and it is his habit to impute unworthy motives to those with whom he differs. Aside from this, however, I shall feel some delicacy in availing myself of a bounty which I was instrumental in persuading the town to vote. Though I feel that I should be perfectly justified in so doing, I confess that I am anxious not to put myself in such a position as to hazard any loss of good opinion on the part of my friends in town."

"Then don't take it," said Mrs. Frost, promptly.

" That's what I say too, father," chimed in Frank.

" Don't decide too hastily," said Mr. Frost. " Remember that in our circumstances this amount of money would be very useful. Although Frank will do as well as any boy of his age, I do not expect him to make the farm as profitable as I should do, partly on account of my experience being greater, and partly because I should be able to accomplish more work than he. One hundred and fifty dollars would procure many little comforts which otherwise you may have to do without."

" I know that," said Mrs. Frost, quickly. " But do you think I should enjoy them, if there were reports circulated, however unjustly, to your prejudice? Besides, I shall know that the comforts at the camp must be fewer than you would enjoy at home. We shall not wish to fare so much better than you."

" Do you think with your mother, Frank?" asked Mr. Frost.

" I think mother is right," said Frank, proud of having his opinion asked. He was secretly determined, in spite of what his father had said, to see if he could not make the farm as profitable as it would be under his father's management.

Mr. Frost seemed relieved by his wife's expression of opinion. " Then," said he, " I will accept your decision as final. I felt that it should be you, and not myself, who should decide it. Now my mind will be at ease, so far as that goes."

"You will not enlist at once, father?" asked Frank.

"Not for three or four weeks. I shall wish to give you some special instructions before I go, so that your task may be easier."

"Had n't I better leave school at once?"

"You may finish this week out. However, I may as well begin my instructions without delay. I believe you have never learned to milk."

"No sir."

"Probably Carter will undertake that. Still, it will be desirable that you should know how, in case he gets sick. You may come out with me after supper and take your first lesson."

Frank ran for his hat with alacrity. This seemed like beginning in earnest. He accompanied his father to the barn, and looked with new interest at the four cows constituting his father's stock.

"I think we will begin with this one," said his father, pointing to a red and white heifer. "She is better-natured than the others, and, as I dare say your fingers will bungle a little at first, that is a point to be considered."

If any of my boy-readers has ever undertaken the task of milking for the first time, he will appreciate Frank's difficulties. When he had seen his father milking, it seemed to him extremely easy. The milk poured out in rich streams, almost without an effort. But under his inexperienced fingers none came. He tugged away manfully, but with no result.

"I guess the cow's dry," said he at last, looking up in his father's face.

Mr. Frost in reply drew out a copious stream.

"I did the same as you," said Frank, mystified, "and none came."

"You did n't take hold right," said his father, "and you pressed at the wrong time. Let me show you."

Before the first lesson was over Frank had advanced a little in the art of milking, and it may as well be said here that in the course of a week or so he became a fair proficient, so that his father even allowed him to try Vixen, a cow who had received this name from the uncertainty of her temper. She had more than once upset the pail with a spiteful kick when it was nearly over. One morning she upset not only the pail but Frank, who looked foolish enough as he got up covered with milk.

Frank also commenced reading the "Ploughman," a weekly agricultural paper which his father had taken for years. Until now he had confined his readings in it to the selected story on the fourth page. Now, with an object in view, he read carefully other parts of the paper. He did this not merely in the first flush of enthusiasm, but with the steady purpose of qualifying himself to take his father's place.

"Frank is an uncommon boy," said Mr. Frost to

5*

his wife, not without feelings of pride, one night when our hero had retired to bed. "I would trust him with the farm sooner than many who are half a dozen years older."

VII

LIKE FATHER, LIKE SON.

"WELL, father, I've got some news for you," said John Haynes, as he entered his father's presence, two or three days later.

"What is it, John?" inquired the Squire, laying down a copy of the New York Herald, which he had been reading.

"Who do you think has enlisted?"

"I do not choose to guess," said his father, coldly. "If you feel disposed to tell me, you may do so."

John looked somewhat offended at his father's tone, but he was anxious to tell the news. "Frost's going to enlist," he said, shortly.

"Indeed!" said the Squire, with interest. "How did you hear?"

"I heard him say so himself, just now, in the store."

"I expected it," said Squire Haynes with a sneer. "I understood his motives perfectly in urging the town to pay an enormous bounty to volunteers. He meant to line his own pockets at the public expense."

"He says that he does n't mean to accept the

bounty," continued John, in a tone which indicated
a doubt whether Mr. Frost was in earnest.

"Did you hear him say that?" asked Squire
Haynes, abruptly.

"Yes. I heard him say so to Mr. Morse."

"Perhaps he means it, and perhaps he does n't.
If he don't take it, it is because he is afraid of public
opinion. What's he going to do about the farm,
while he is gone?"

"That is the strangest part of it," said John. "I
don't believe you could guess who is to be left in
charge of it."

"I don't choose to guess. If you know, speak
out."

John bit his lip resentfully.

"It's that conceited jackanapes of his, — Frank
Frost."

"Do you mean that he is going to leave that boy
to carry on the farm?" demanded Squire Haynes, in
surprise.

"Yes."

"Well, all I can say is, that he's more of a fool
than I took him to be."

"O, he thinks everything of Frank," said John,
bitterly. "He'll be nominating him for Representative, next."

The Squire winced a little. He had been ambitious to represent the town in the Legislature, and
after considerable wire-pulling, had succeeded in

obtaining the nomination the year previous. But it is one thing to be nominated and another to be elected. So the Squire had found, to his cost. He had barely obtained fifty votes, while his opponent had been elected by a vote of a hundred and fifty. All allusions, therefore, recalling his mortifying defeat, were disagreeable to him.

"On the whole, I don't know but I am satisfied," he said, recurring to the intelligence John had brought. "So far as I am concerned, I am glad he has made choice of this boy."

"You don't think he is competent?" asked John, in surprise.

"For that very reason I am glad he has been selected," said the Squire, emphatically. "I take it for granted that the farm will be mismanaged, and become a bill of expense instead of a source of revenue. It's pretty certain that Frost won't be able to pay the mortgage when it comes due. I can bid off the farm for a small sum additional, and make a capital bargain. It will make a very good place for you to settle down upon, John."

"Me!" said John, disdainfully. "You don't expect me to become a plodding farmer, I trust. I've got talent for something better than that, I should hope."

"No," said the Squire, "I have other views for you. Still, you could hire a farmer to carry it on for you, and live out there in the summer."

" Well, perhaps that would do," said John, thinking that it would sound well for him, even if he lived
in the city, to have a place in the country.   " When
does the mortgage come due, father ? "

" I don't remember the exact date.   I 'll look and
see."

The Squire drew from a closet a box hooped with
iron, and evidently made for security.   This was his
strong box, and in this he kept his bonds, mortgages,
and other securities.

He selected a document tied with red ribbon, and
examined it briefly.

" I shall have the right to foreclose the mortgage
on the first of next July," he said.

" I hope you will do it then.   I should like to see
them Frosts humbled."

" *Them* Frosts !   Don't you know anything more
about English grammar, John ? "

" Those Frosts, then.   Of course I know; but a
feller can't always be watching his words."

" I desire you never again to use the low word
' feller,' " said the Squire, who, as the reader will
see, was more particular about grammatical accuracy
than about some other things which might be naturally supposed to be of higher importance.

" Well," said John, sulkily, " anything you
choose."

" As to the mortgage," proceeded Squire Haynes,
" I have no idea they will be able to lift it.   I feel

certain that Frost wont himself have the money at command; and I shan't give him any grace, or consent to a renewal. He may be pretty sure of that."

"Perhaps he'll find somebody to lend him the money."

"I think not. There are those who would be willing; but I question whether there is any such who could raise the money at a moment's warning. By the way, you need not mention my purpose in this matter to any one. If it should leak out, Mr. Frost might hear of it, and prepare for it."

"You may trust me for that, father," said John, very decidedly; "I want to see Frank Frost's proud spirit humbled. Perhaps he'll feel like putting on airs after that."

From the conversation which has just been chronicled, it will be perceived that John was a worthy son of his father; and, though wanting in affection and cordial good feeling, that both were prepared to join hands in devising mischief to poor Frank and his family. Let us hope that the intentions of the wicked may be frustrated. .

VIII.

DISCOURAGED AND ENCOURAGED.

In a small village like Rossville news flies fast. Even the distinctions of social life do not hinder an interest being felt in the affairs of each individual. Hence it was that Mr. Frost's determination to enlist became speedily known; and various were the comments made upon his plan of leaving Frank in charge of the farm. That they were not all favorable may be readily believed. Country people are apt to criticise the proceedings of their neighbors with a greater degree of freedom than is common elsewhere.

As Frank was on his way to school on Saturday morning, his name was called by Mrs Roxana Mason, who stood in the doorway of a small yellow house fronting on the main street.

"Good morning, Mrs. Mason," said Frank, politely, advancing to the gate in answer to her call.

"Is it true what I've heard about your father's going to the war, Frank Frost?" she commenced.

"Yes, Mrs. Mason; he feels it his duty to go."

"And what's to become of the farm? anybody hired it?"

"I am going to take charge of it," said Frank, modestly.

"You!" exclaimed Mrs. Roxana, lifting both hands in amazement; "why, you're nothing but a baby!"

"I'm a baby of fifteen," said Frank, good humoredly, though his courage was a little damped by her tone.

"What do you know about farming?" inquired the lady, in a contemptuous manner. "Your father must be crazy!"

"I shall do my best, Mrs. Mason," said Frank, quietly, but with heightened color. "My father is willing to trust me; and as I shall have Mr. Maynard to look to for advice, I think I can get along."

"The idea of putting a boy like you over a farm!" returned Mrs. Roxana, in an uncompromising tone. "I did think your father had more sense. It's the most shiftless thing I ever knew him to do. How does your poor mother feel about it?"

"She doesn't seem as much disturbed about it as you do, Mrs. Mason," said Frank, rather impatiently; for he felt that Mrs. Mason had no right to interfere in his father's arrangements.

"Well, well, we'll see!" said Mrs. Roxana, shaking her head significantly. "If you'll look in your Bible, you'll read about 'the haughty spirit that goes before a fall.' I'm sure I wish you well

6

enough. I hope that things'll turn out better'n they're like to. Tell your mother I'll come over before long and talk with her about it."

Frank inwardly hoped that Mrs. Roxana would n't put herself to any trouble to call; but politeness taught him to be silent.

Leaving Mrs. Mason's gate he kept on his way to school, but had hardly gone half a dozen rods before he met an old lady, whose benevolent face indicated a very different disposition from that of the lady he had just parted with.

" Good morning, Mrs. Chester," said Frank, cordially, recognizing one of his mother's oldest friends.

" Good morning, my dear boy," was the reply. " I hear your father is going to the war."

" Yes," said Frank, a little nervously, not knowing but Mrs. Chester would view the matter ·in the same way with Mrs. Mason, though he felt sure she would express herself less disagreeably.

" And I hear that you are going to try to make his place good at home."

" I don't expect to make his place good, Mrs. Chester," said Frank, modestly; " but I shall do as well as I can."

" I have no doubt of it, my dear boy," said the old lady, kindly. " You can do a great deal, too. You can help your mother by looking out for your brothers and sisters, as well as supplying your father's place on the farm."

" I am glad you think I can make myself useful,"
said Frank, feeling relieved. " Mrs. Mason has just
been telling me that I am not fit for the charge, and
that discouraged me a little."

" It's a great responsibility, no doubt, to come
on one so young," said the old lady; " but it's of
God's appointing. He will strengthen your hands,
if you only ask Him. If you humbly seek his guidance and assistance, you need not fear to fail."

" Yes," said Frank, soberly; " that's what I
mean to do."

" Then you will feel that you are in the path of
duty. You'll be serving your country just as much
as if you went yourself."

" That's just the way I feel, Mrs. Chester,"
exclaimed Frank, eagerly. " I want to do something for my country."

" You remind me of my oldest brother," said the
old lady, thoughtfully. " He was left pretty much
as you are. It was about the middle of the Revolu-
tionary war, and the army needed recruits. My
father hesitated, for he had a small family depending
on him for support. I was only two years old at the
time, and there were three others of us. Finally my
brother James, who was just about your age, told
my father that he would do all he could to support
the family, and father concluded to go. We did n't
have a farm, for father was a carpenter. My brother
worked for neighboring farmers, receiving his pay in

corn and vegetables, and picked up what odd jobs he
could.   Then mother was able to do something; so
we managed after a fashion.   There were times when
we were brought pretty close to the wall; but God
carried us through.   And by-and-by father came
safely home, and I don't think he ever regretted having left us.   After a while the good news of peace
came, and he felt that he had been abundantly repaid
_for all the sacrifices he had made in the good cause."

Frank listened to this narrative with great interest.
It yielded him no little encouragement to know that
another boy, placed in similar circumstances, had
succeeded, and he justly felt that he would have very
much less to contend against than the brother of
whom Mrs. Chester spoke.

"Thank you for telling me about your brother,
Mrs. Chester," he said.   "It makes me feel more as
if things would turn out well.   Won't you come over
soon and see us?   Mother is always glad to see you."

"Thank you, Frank; I shall certainly do so.   I
hope I shall not make you late to school."

"O no; I started half an hour early this morning."

Frank had hardly left Mrs. Chester when he heard
a quick step behind him.   Turning round he perceived that it was Mr. Rathburn, his teacher.

"I hurried to come up with you, Frank," he said,
smiling.   "I understand that I am to lose you from
school."

"Yes, sir," answered Frank. "I am very sorry to leave, for I am very much interested in my studies; but I suppose, sir, you have heard what calls me away."

"Your father has made up his mind to enlist."

"Yes, sir."

"And you are to superintend the farm in his absence?"

"Yes, sir. I hope you do not think me presumptuous in undertaking such a responsibility?"

He looked up eagerly into Mr. Rathburn's face, for he had a great respect for his judgment. But he saw nothing to discourage him. On the contrary he read cordial sympathy and approval.

"Far from it," answered the teacher, with emphasis. "I think you deserving of great commendation, especially if, as I have heard, the plan originated with you, and was by you suggested to your father."

"Yes, sir."

The teacher held out his hand kindly. "It was only what I should have expected of you," he said. "I have not forgotten your essay. I am glad to see that you not only have right ideas of duty, but have, what is rarer, the courage and self-denial to put them in practice."

These words gave Frank much pleasure, and his face lighted up.

"Shall you feel obliged to give up your studies entirely?" asked his teacher.

6*

I think I shall be able to study some in the evening."

"If I can be of any assistance to you in any way, don't hesitate to apply. If you should find any stumbling-blocks in your lessons, I may be able to help you over them."

By this time they had come within sight of the schoolhouse.

"There comes the young farmer," said John Haynes, in a tone which was only subdued lest the teacher should hear him, for he had no disposition to incur another public rebuke.

A few minutes later, when Frank was quietly seated at his desk, a paper was thrown from behind lighting upon his Virgil, which lay open before him. There appeared to be writing upon it, and with some curiosity he opened and read the following! "What's the price of turnips?"

It was quite unnecessary to inquire into the authorship. He felt confident that it was written by John Haynes. The latter of course intended it as an insult, but Frank did not feel much disturbed. As long as his conduct was approved by such persons as his teacher and Mrs. Chester, he felt that he could safely disregard the taunts and criticisms of others. He therefore quietly let the paper drop to the floor, and kept on with his lesson.

John Haynes perceived that he had failed in his benevolent purpose of disturbing Frank's tranquillity, and this, I am sorry to say, only increased the dislike which he felt for him. Nothing is so unreasonable as anger, nothing so hard to appease. John even felt disposed to regard as an insult the disposition which Frank had made of his insulting query.

"The young clodhopper's on his dignity," he muttered to himself. "Well, wait a few months, and see if he won't sing a different tune."

Just then John's class was called up, and his dislike to Frank was not diminished by the superiority of his recitation. The latter, undisturbed by John's feelings, did not give a thought to him, but reflected with a touch of pain that this must be his last Latin recitation in school for a long time to come.

IX.

THE LAST EVENING AT HOME.

THREE weeks passed quickly. October had already reached its middle point. The glory of the Indian summer was close at hand. Too quickly the days fled for the little family at the farm, for they knew that each brought nearer the parting of which they could not bear to think.

Jacob Carter, who had been sent for to do the heavy work on the farm, had arrived. He was a man of forty, stout and able to work, but had enjoyed few opportunities of cultivating his mind. Though a faithful laborer, he was destitute of the energy and ambition which might ere this have placed him in charge of a farm of his own. In New England few arrive at his age without achieving some position more desirable and independent than that of farm laborer. However, he looked pleasant and good natured, and Mr. Frost accounted himself fortunate in securing his services.

The harvest had been got in, and during the winter months there would not be so much to do as before. Jacob, therefore, " hired out " for a smaller compensation, to be increased when the spring work came in.

Frank had not been idle. He had accompanied his father about the farm, and received as much practical instruction in the art of farming as the time would admit. He was naturally a quick learner, and now felt impelled by a double motive to prepare himself as well as possible to assume his new responsibilities. His first motive was of course to make up his father's loss to the family, as far as it was possible for him to do so, but he was also desirous of showing Mrs. Roxana Mason, and other ill-boding prophets, that they had underrated his abilities.

The time came when Mr. Frost felt that he must leave his family. He had enlisted from preference in an old regiment, already in Virginia, some members of which had gone from Rossville. A number of recruits were to be forwarded to the camp on a certain day, and that day was now close at hand.

Let me introduce the reader to the farmhouse on the last evening for many months when they would be able to be together. They were all assembled about the fireplace. Mr. Frost sat in an arm-chair, holding Charlie in his lap, — the privileged place of the youngest. Alice, with the air of a young woman sat demurely by her father's side on a cricket, while Maggie stood beside him with one hand resting on his knee. Frank sat quietly beside his mother, as if already occupying the place which he was in future to hold as her counsellor and protector.

Frank and his mother looked sober. They had not realized fully until this evening what it would be to part with the husband and father, — how constantly they would miss him at the family meal and in the evening circle. Then there was the dreadful uncertainty of war. He might never return, or, if spared for that, it might be with a broken constitution or the loss of a limb.

" If it hadn't been for me," Frank could not help thinking, " father would not now be going away. He would have stayed at home, and I could still go to school. It would have made a great difference to us, and the loss of one man could not affect the general result."

A moment after his conscience rebuked him for harboring so selfish a thought.

" The country needs him more even than we do," he said to himself. " It will be a hard trial to have him go, but it is our duty."

" Will my little Charlie miss me when I am gone ? " asked Mr. Frost of the chubby-faced boy who sat with great round eyes peering into the fire, as if he were deeply engaged in thought.

" Won't you take me with you, papa ? " asked Charlie.

" What could you do, if you were out there, my little boy ? " asked the father, smiling.

"I'd shoot great big rebel with my gun," said Charlie, waxing valiant.

"Your gun's only a wooden one," said Maggie, with an air of superior knowledge. "You couldn't kill a rebel with that."

"I'd kill 'em *some*," persisted Charlie, earnestly, — evidently believing that a wooden gun differed from others not in kind but in degree.

"But suppose the rebels should fire at you," said Frank, amused. "What would you do then, Charlie?"

Charlie looked into the fire thoughtfully for a moment, as if this contingency had not presented itself to his mind until now. Suddenly his face brightened up, and he answered, "I'd run away just as fast as I could."

All laughed at this, and Frank said, "but that wouldn't be acting like a brave soldier, Charlie. You ought to stay, and make the enemy run."

"I wouldn't want to stay and be *shooted*," said Charlie, ingenuously.

"There are many older than Charlie," said Mr. Frost, smiling, "who would doubtless sympathize entirely with him in his objection to being *shooted*, though they might not be quite so ready to make confession as he has shown himself. I suppose you have heard the couplet, —

'He who fights and runs away,
May live to fight another day.'

"Pray don't speak about shooting," said Mrs. Frost with a shudder. "It makes me feel nervous."

"And to-night we should only admit pleasant thoughts," said her husband. "Who is going to write me letters when I am gone?"

"I'll write to you father," said Alice.

"And so will I," said Maggie.

"I too," chimed in Charlie.

"Then if you have so many correspondents already engaged, you will hardly want to hear from Frank and myself," said his wife, smiling.

"The more the better. I suspect I shall find letters more welcome than anything else. You must also send me papers regularly. I shall have many hours that will pass heavily unless I have something to read."

"I'll mail you Harper's Weekly regularly, shall I, father?" asked Frank.

"Yes, I shall be glad enough to see it. Then, there is one good thing about papers, after enjoying them myself I can pass them round to others. There are many privations that I must make up my mind to, but I shall endeavor to make camp-life as pleasant as possible to myself and others."

"I wish you were going out as an officer," said Mrs. Frost. "You would have more indulgences."

"Very probably I should. But I don't feel inclined to wish myself better off than others. I am willing to serve my country in any capacity in which

I can be of use. Thank Heaven, I am pretty strong
and healthy, and better fitted than many to encounter
the fatigues and exposures which are the lot of the
private."

" How early must you start to-morrow, father?"
inquired Frank.

" By daylight. I must be in Boston by nine
o'clock, and you know it is a five-mile ride to the
depot. I shall want you to carry me over."

" Will there be room for me?" asked Mrs. Frost.
" I want to see the last of you."

" I hope you won't do that for a long time to
come," said Mr. Frost, smiling.

" You know what I mean, Henry."

" O yes, there will be room. At any rate, we
will make room for you. And now it seems to me
it is time for these little folks to go to bed. Charlie
finds it hard work to keep his eyes open."

" O papa, papa, not yet, not yet," pleaded the
children; and with the thought that it might be
many a long day before he saw their sweet young
faces again, the father suffered them to have their
way.

After the children had fairly gone to bed Frank
and his father and mother sat up for a long time.
Each felt that there was much to be said; but no one
of them felt like saying much then. Thoughts of the
approaching separation swallowed up all others. The
thought kept recurring that to-morrow would see

7

them many miles apart, and that many a long to-morrow must pass before they would again be gathered around the fire.

"Frank," said his father, at length, "I have deposited in the Brandon Bank four hundred dollars, about half of which I have realized from crops sold this season. This you will draw upon as you have need, for grocery bills, to pay Jacob, &c. For present purposes I will hand you fifty dollars, which I advise you to put under your mother's care.

As he finished speaking, Mr. Frost, drew from his pocket-book a roll of bills, and handed them to Frank.

Frank opened his porte-monnaie and deposited the money therein.

He had never before so large a sum in his possession, and although he knew it was not to be spent for his own benefit, — at least, no considerable part of it, — he felt a sense of importance and even wealth in being the custodian of so much money. He felt that his father had confidence in him, and that he was in truth going to be his representative.

"A part of the money which I have in the Bank," continued his father, "has been saved up towards the payment of the mortgage on the farm."

"When does it come due, father?"

"On the first of July of next year."

"But you won't be prepared to meet it at that time?"

" No, but undoubtedly Squire Haynes will be willing to renew it. I always pay the interest promptly, and he knows it is secured by the farm, and therefore a safe investment. By the way, I had nearly forgotten to say that there will be some interest due on the first of January. Of course, you are authorized to pay it just as if you were myself."

" How much will it be ? "

" Twenty-four dollars ; that is, six months interest at six per cent on eight hundred dollars."

" I wish the farm were free from incumbrance," said Frank.

" So do I ; and if providence favors me it shall be before many years are past. But in farming one can't expect to lay by money quite as fast as in some other employments."

The old clock in the corner here struck eleven.

" We must n't keep you up too late the last night, Henry," said Mrs. Frost, " you will need a good night's sleep to carry you through to-morrow."

Neither of the three closed their eyes early that night. Thoughts of the morrow were naturally in their minds. But at last all was still. Sleep — God's beneficent messenger — wrapt their senses in oblivion, and the cares and anxieties of the morrow were for a time forgotten.

X.

LITTLE POMP.

THERE was a hurried good by at the depot.

"Kiss the children for me, Mary," said her husband.

"You will write *very* soon," pleaded Mr. Frost.

"By the very first opportunity."

"All aboard!" shouted the conductor.

With a shrill scream the locomotive started.

Frank and his mother stood on the platform watching the receding train till it was quite out of sight, and then in silence our young hero assisted his mother into the carryall, and turned the horse's head homewards.

It was one of those quiet October mornings, when the air is soft and balmy as if a June day had found its way by mistake into the heart of autumn. The road wound partly through the woods. The leaves were still green and abundant. Only one or two showed signs of the coming change, which in the course of a few weeks must leave them bare and leafless.

"What a beautiful day!" said Frank, speaking the words almost unconsciously.

" Beautiful indeed ! " responded his mother. " On such a day as this the world seems too lovely for war and warlike passions to be permitted to enter it. When men might be so happy, why need they stain their hands with each others' blood ? "

Frank was unprepared for an answer. He knew that it was his father's departure which led his mother to speak thus. He wished to divert her mind if possible.

Circumstances favored his design.

They had accomplished, perhaps, three quarters of the distance home, when, as they were passing a small one story building by the roadside, a shriek of pain was heard, and a little black boy came running out of the house screaming in affright, — " Mammy's done killed herself. She's mos' dead ! "

He ran out to the road, and looked up at Mrs. Frost, as if to implore assistance.

" That's Chloe's child," said Mrs. Frost. " Stop the horse, Frank ; I'll get out and see what has happened."

Chloe, as Frank very well knew, was a colored woman, who until a few months since had been a slave in Virginia. Finally, she had seized a favorable opportunity, and taking the only child which the cruel slave system had left her, for the rest had been sold South, succeeded in making her way into Pennsylvania. Chance had directed her to Rossville, where she had been permitted to occupy rent-free an old shanty which for some years previous had been un-inhabited. Here she had supported herself by taking in washing and ironing. This had been her special work on the plantation where she had been born and brought up, and she was therefore quite proficient in it. She found no difficulty in obtaining work enough to satisfy the moderate wants of herself and little Pomp.

The latter was a bright little fellow, as black as the ace of spades, and possessing to the full the mercurial temperament of the Southern negro. Full of fun and drollery, he attracted plenty of attention when he came into the village, and earned many a penny from the boys by his plantation songs and dances.

Now, however, he appeared in a mood entirely different, and it was easy to see that he was much frightened.

"What's the matter, Pomp?" asked Frank, as he brought his horse to a stand-still.

"Mammy done killed herself," he repeated, wringing his hands in terror.

A moan from the interior of the house seemed to make it clear that something had happened.

Mrs. Frost pushed the door open and entered.

Chloe had sunk down on the floor, and was rocking back and forth, holding her right foot in both hands, with an expression of acute pain on her sable face. Beside her was a small pail bottom upwards.

Mrs Frost was at no loss to conjecture the nature of the accident which had befallen her. The pail had contained hot water, and its accidental overturn had scalded poor Chloe.

"Are you much hurt, Chloe?" asked Mrs. Frost, sympathizingly.

"O missus, I 'se most dead," was the reply, accompanied by a groan. "Spect I shan't live till mornin'. Dunno what 'll become of poor Pomp when I 'se gone."

Little Pomp squeezed his knuckles into his eyes, and responded with an unearthly howl.

"Don't be too much frightened, Chloe," said Mrs. Frost, soothingly. "You 'll get over it sooner than you think. How did the pail happen to turn over?"

"Must have been de debble, missus. I was kerryin it just as keerful when all at once it upsot."

This explanation, though not very luminous to her visitor, appeared to excite a fierce spirit of resentment against the pail in the mind of little Pomp.

He suddenly rushed forward impetuously and kicked the pail with all the force he could muster.

But alas for poor Pomp! His feet were unprotected by shoes, and the sudden blow hurt him much more than the pail. The consequence was a howl of the most distressing nature.

Frank had started forward to rescue Pomp from the consequences of his precipitancy, but too late. He picked up the little fellow, and carrying him out strove to soothe him.

Meanwhile, Mrs. Frost examined Chloe's injuries. They were not so great as she had anticipated. She learned on inquiry that the water had not been scalding hot. There was little doubt that with proper care she would recover from her injuries in a week or ten days. But in the mean time it would not do to use the foot.

"What shall I do, missus?" groaned Chloe. "I ain't got nothin' baked up. 'Pears like me and Pomp must starve."

"Not so bad as that, Chloe," said Mrs. Frost, with a reassuring smile. "After we have you on the bed we will take Pomp home with us, and give him enough food to last you both a couple of days. At the end of that time, or sooner if you get out, you can send him up again."

Chloe expressed her gratitude warmly, and Mrs. Frost, calling in Frank's assistance, helped the poor woman to a comfortable position on the bed, which fortunately was in the corner of the same room. Had it been up stairs the removal would have been attended with considerable difficulty as well as pain to Chloe.

Pomp, the acuteness of whose pain had subsided, looked on with wondering eyes, while Frank and Mrs. Frost "toted" his mother on to the bed, as he expressed it.

Chloe accepted, with wondering gratitude, the personal attentions of Mrs. Frost, who bound up the in jured foot with a softness of touch which brought no pain to the sufferer.

"You ain't too proud, missus, to tend a poor black woman," she said. "Down Souf dey used to tell us dat everybody looked down on de poor nigger and lef' 'em to starve an' die if dey grow sick."

"They told you a great many things that were not true, Chloe," said Mrs. Frost, quietly. "The color of the skin ought to make no difference where we have it in our power to render kind offices."

"Do you believe niggers go to de same heaven wid wite folks, missus?" asked Chloe, after a pause.

"Why should they not? They were made by the same God."

"I dunno, missus," said Chloe. "I hopes you is right."

"Do you think you can spare Pomp a little while to go home with us?"

"Yes, missus. Here you Pomp," she called, "you go home wid dis good lady, and she'll gib you something for your poor sick mudder. Do you hear?"

"I'se goin' to ride?" said Pomp, inquiringly.

"Yes," said Frank, good-naturedly.

"Hi, hi, dat's prime!" ejaculated Pomp, turning a somerset, in his joy.

"Scramble in, then, and we'll start."

Pomp needed no second invitation. He jumped into the carriage, and was more leisurely followed by Frank and his mother.

It was probably the first time that Pomp had ever been in a covered carriage, and consequently the novelty of his situation put him in high spirits.

He was anxious to drive, and Frank, to gratify him, placed the reins in his hands. His eyes sparkling with delight, and his expanded mouth showing a full set of ivories, Pomp shook the reins in glee, shouting out, " Hi, go long there, you ol' debble ! '

" Pomp, you must n't use that word," said Mrs. Frost, reprovingly.

" What word, missus ? " demanded Pomp, innocently.

" The last word you used," she answered.

" Don't 'member what word you mean, missus," said Pomp. " Hi, you debble ! "

" That's the word ? "

" Not say debble ? " said Pomp, wonderingly. " Why not, missus ? "

" It is n't a good word."

" Mammy says debble. She calls me little debble when I run away, and don't tote in de wood."

" I shall tell her not to use it. It is n't a good word for anybody to use."

" Hope you 'll tell her so, missus," said Pomp, grinning and showing his teeth. " Wheneber she calls me little debble, she pulls off her shoe and hits me. Hurts like de debble. Mebbe she won't hit me if you tell her not to say debble."

Mrs. Frost could hardly forbear laughing. She

managed, however, to preserve a serious countenance while she said, "You must take care to behave well, and then she won't have to punish you."

It is somewhat doubtful whether Pomp heard this last remark. He espied a pig walking by the side of the road, and was seized with the desire to run over it. Giving the reins a sudden twitch, he brought the carriage round so that it was very near upsetting in a gully.

Frank snatched the reins in time to prevent this catastrophe.

"What did you do that for, Pomp?" he said, quickly.

"Wanted to scare de pig," exclaimed Pomp, laughing. "Wanted to hear him squeal."

"And so you nearly tipped us over."

"Did n't mean to do dat, Mass Frank. 'Pears like I did n't think."

Mrs. Frost was too much alarmed by this narrow escape to consent to Pomp's driving again, and for the moment felt as if she should like to usurp his mother's privilege of spanking him. But the little imp looked so unconscious of having done anything wrong, that her vexation soon passed away.

In half an hour Pomp was on his way back, laden with a basket full of provisions for his sick mother and himself.

XI.

PUNISHING A BULLY.

IT was fortunate for Mrs. Frost that she was so soon called upon to think for others. It gave her less time to grieve over her husband's absence, which was naturally a severe trial to her. As for Frank, though the harvest was gathered in, there were plenty of small jobs to occupy his attention. He divided with Jacob the care of the cows, and was up betimes in the morning to do his share of the milking. Then the pigs and chickens must be fed every day, and this Frank took entirely into his own charge. Wood, also, must be prepared for the daily wants of the house, and this labor he shared with Jacob.

In the afternoon, however, Frank usually had two or three hours at his own disposal, and this, in accordance with a previous determination, he resolved to devote to keeping up his studies. He did not expect to make the same progress that he would have done if he had been able to continue at school, but it was something to feel that he was not remaining stationary.

Frank resolved to say nothing to his classmates

about his private studies. They would think he was falling far behind, and at some future time he would surprise them.

Still, there were times when he felt the need of a teacher. He would occasionally encounter difficulties which he found himself unable to surmount without assistance. At such times he thought of Mr. Rathburn's kind offer. But his old teacher lived nearly a mile distant, and he felt averse to troubling him, knowing that his duties in school were arduous.

Occasionally he met some of his schoolmates. As nearly all of them were friendly and well disposed to him, this gave him pleasure, and brought back sometimes the wish that he was as free as they. But this wish was almost instantly checked by the thought that he had made a sacrifice for his country's sake.

A few days after the incident narrated in the last chapter, Frank was out in the woods not far from Chloe's cottage, collecting brushwood, to be afterwards carried home, when his attention was called to an altercation, one of the parties in which he readily recognized as little Pomp. To explain how it came about, we shall have to go back a little.

Pomp was returning from Mrs. Frost's, swinging a tin-kettle containing provisions for his mother and himself, when all at once he met John Haynes, who was coming from the opposite direction.

Now, John was something of a bully, and liked to exercise authority over boys who were small enough to render the attempt a safe one. On the present occasion he felt in a hectoring mood.

"I'll have some fun out of the little nigger," he said to himself, as he espied Pomp.

Pomp approached, swinging his pail as before, and whistling a plantation melody.

"What have you got there, Pomp?" asked John.

"I'se got a pail," said Pomp, independently. "Don't yer know a pail when you see him?"

"I know an impudent little nigger when I see him," retorted John, not over pleased with the answer. "Come here directly, and let me see what you've got in your pail."

"I ain't got noffin for you," said Pomp, defiantly.

"We'll see about that," said John. "Now do you mean to come here or not? I'm going to count three, and I'll give you till that time to decide. One — two — three!"

Pomp apparently had no intention of complying with John's request. He had halted about three rods from him, and stood swinging his pail, meanwhile watching John warily.

"I see you want me to come after you," said John, angrily.

He ran towards Pomp, but the little contraband dodged him adroitly, and got on the other side of a tree.

Opposition only stimulated John to new efforts. He had become excited in the pursuit, and had made up his mind to capture Pomp. He dodged in and out among the trees with such quickness and dexterity that John was foiled for a considerable time. The ardor of his pursuit and its unexpected difficulty excited his anger. He lost sight of the fact that Pomp was under no obligation to comply with his demand. But this is generally the way with tyrants, who are seldom careful to keep within the bounds of justice and reason.

"Just let me catch you, you little rascal, and I will give you the worst licking you ever had," John exclaimed, with passion.

"Wait till you catch me," returned Pomp, slipping eel-like from his grasp.

But Pomp, in dodging, had now come to an open space, where he was at disadvantage. John was close upon him, when suddenly he stood stock still, bending his back so as to obtain a firm footing. The consequence was, that his too ardent pursuer tumbled over him, and stretched his length upon the ground.

Unfortunately for Pomp, John grasped his leg in falling, and held it by so firm a grip that he was unable to get free. In the moment of his downfall John attained his object.

"Now I've got you," he said, white with passion, "and I'm going to teach you a lesson."

Clinging to Pomp with one hand, he drew a stout

string from his pocket with the other, and secured
the hands of the little contraband, notwithstanding
his efforts to escape.

" Le' me go, you debble," he said, using a word
which had grown familiar to him on the plantation.

There was a cruel light in John's eyes which au-
gured little good to poor Pomp. Suddenly, as if a
new idea had struck him, he loosened the cord, and
taking the boy carried him in spite of his kicking and
screaming to a small tree, around which he clasped
his hands which he again confined with cords.

He then sought out a stout stick, and divested it
of twigs.

Pomp watched his preparations with terror. Too
well he knew what they meant. More than once he
had seen those of his own color whipped on the plantation. Unconsciously he glided into the language
which he would have used there.

" Don't whip me, massa John," he whimpered in
terror. " For the lub of heaven lef' me be. I ain't
done noffin to you."

" You 'd better have thought of that before," said
John, his eyes blazing anew with vengeful light.
" If I whip you, you little black rascal, it 's only
because you richly deserve it."

" I 'll nebber do so again," pleaded Pomp, rolling
his eyes in terror. Though what it was he promised
not to do the poor little fellow would have found it
hard to tell.

It would have been as easy to soften the heart of a nether millstone as that of John Haynes.

By the time he had completed his preparations, and whirled his stick in the air preparatory to bringing it down with full force on Pomp's back, rapid steps were heard, and a quick voice asked, "what are you doing there, John Haynes?"

John looked round, and saw standing near him Frank Frost, whose attention had been excited by what he had heard of Pomp's cries.

"Save me, save me, Mass Frank," pleaded poor little Pomp.

"What has he tied you up there for, Pomp?"

"It's none of your business, Frank Frost," said John, passionately.

"I think it's some of my business," said Frank, coolly, "when I find you playing the part of a Southern overseer. You are not in Richmond, John Haynes, and you'll get into trouble if you undertake to act as if you were."

"If you say much more, I'll flog you too!" screamed John, beside himself with excitement and rage.

Frank had not a particle of cowardice in his composition. He was not fond of fighting, but he felt that circumstances made it necessary for him to do so now. He did not easily lose his temper, and this at present gave him the advantage over John.

"You are too excited to know what you are talk-

8*

ing about," he said, coolly. "Pomp, why has he tied you up?"

Pomp explained that John had tried to get his pail from him. He closed by imploring "Mass Frank" to prevent John from whipping him.

"He shall not whip you, Pomp," said Frank, quietly. As he spoke he stepped to the tree, and faced John intrepidly.

John, in a moment of less passion, would not have ventured to attack a boy so near his own size. Like all bullies he was essentially a coward; but now his rage got the better of his prudence.

"I'll flog you both!" he exclaimed, hoarsely, and sprang forward with upraised stick.

Frank was about half a head shorter than John, and was more than a year younger, but he was stout and compactly built; besides, he was cool and collected, and this is always an advantage.

Before John realized what had happened, his stick had flown from his hand, and he was forcibly pushed back so that he narrowly escaped falling to the ground.

"Gib it to him, Mass Frank!" shouted little Pomp; "gib it to him!"

This increased John's exasperation. By this time he was almost foaming at the mouth.

"I'll kill you, Frank Frost," he exclaimed, this time rushing at him without a stick.

Frank had been in the habit of wrestling for sport

with boys of his own size. In this way he had acquired a certain amount of dexterity in " tripping up." John, on the contrary, was unpractised. His quick temper was so easily roused that other boys had declined engaging in friendly contests with him, knowing that in most cases they would degenerate into a fight.

John rushed forward, and attempted to throw Frank by the strength of his arms alone. Frank eluded his grasp, and getting one of his legs around John's, with a quick movement tripped him up. He fell heavily upon his back.

" This is all foolish, John," said Frank, bending over his fallen foe. " What are you fighting for? The privilege of savagely whipping a poor little fellow less than half your age."

" I care more about whipping you, a cursed sight !" said John, taking advantage of Frank's withdrawing his pressure to spring to his feet. " You first, and him afterwards !"

Again he threw himself upon Frank ; but again coolness and practice prevailed against blind fury and untaught strength, and again he lay prostrate.

By this time Pomp had freed himself from the string that fettered his wrists, and danced in glee round John Haynes, in whose discomfiture he felt great delight.

" You 'd better pick up your pail and run home," aid Frank. He was generously desirous of saving

John from further humiliation. "Will you go away quietly if I will let you up, John?" he asked.

"No, d—— you!" returned John, writhing, his face almost livid with passion.

"I am sorry," said Frank, "for in that case I must continue to hold you down."

"What is the trouble, boys?" came from an un-expected quarter.

It was Mr. Maynard, who, chancing to pass along the road, had been attracted by the noise of the struggle.

Frank explained in a few words.

"Let him up, Frank," said the old man. "I'll see that he does no further harm."

John rose to his feet, and looked scowlingly from one to the other, as if undecided whether he had not better attack both.

"You've disgraced yourself, John Haynes," said the old farmer, scornfully. "So you would turn negro-whipper, would you? Your talents are misap-plied here at the North. Brutality isn't respectable here, my lad. You'd better find your way within the Rebel lines, and then perhaps you can gratify your propensity for whipping the helpless."

"Some day I'll be revenged on you for this," said John, turning wrathfully upon Frank. "Perhaps you think I don't mean it, but the day will come when you'll remember what I say."

"I wish you no harm, John," said Frank, com-

posedly, " but I shan't stand by and see you beat a
boy like Pomp."

" No," said the farmer, sternly; " and if ever I
hear of your doing it, I'll horsewhip you till you beg
for mercy. Now go home, and carry your disgrace
with you."

Mr. Maynard spoke contemptuously, but with decision, and pointed up the road.

With smothered wrath John obeyed his order, because he saw that it would not be safe to refuse.

" I'll come up with him yet," he muttered to himself, as he walked quietly towards home. " If he
does n't rue this day, my name is n't John Haynes."

John did not see fit to make known the circumstances of his quarrel with Frank, feeling justly, that
neither his design nor the result would reflect any
credit upon himself. But his wrath was none the
less deep because he brooded over it in secret. He
would have renewed his attempt upon Pomp, but
there was something in Mr. Maynard's eye which
assured him that his threat would be carried out.
Frank, solicitous for the little fellow's safety, kept
vigilant watch over him for some days, but no vio-
lence was attempted. He hoped John had forgotten
his threats.

XII.

A LETTER FROM THE CAMP.

THE little family at the Frost Farm looked forward with anxious eagerness to the first letter from the absent father.

Ten days had elapsed when Frank was seen hurrying up the road with something in his hand.

Alice saw him first, and ran in, exclaiming, "Mother, I do believe Frank has got a letter from father. He is running up the road."

Mrs. Frost at once dropped her work, no less interested than her daughter, and was at the door just as Frank, flushed with running, reached the gate.

"What'll you give for a letter?" he asked, triumphantly.

"Give it to me quick," said Mrs. Frost. "I am anxious to learn whether your father is well."

"I guess he is, or he would n't have written such a long letter."

"How do you know it's long?" asked Alice. "You have n't read it."

"I judge from the weight. There are two stamps

on the envelope. I was tempted to open it, but being directed to mother, I did n't venture."

Mrs. Frost sat down, and the children gathered round her, while she read the following letter : —

CAMP ————, Virginia.

DEAR MARY : —

When I look about me, and consider the novelty and strangeness of my surroundings, I can hardly realize that it is only a week since I sat in our quiet sitting-room at the Farm, with you and our own dear ones around me. I will try to help your imagination to a picture of my present home.

But first let me speak of my journey hither.

It was tedious enough, travelling all day by rail. Of course, little liberty was allowed us. Military discipline is rigid, and must be maintained. Of its necessity we had a convincing proof at a small station between Hartford and New Haven. One of our number, who, I accidentally learned, is a Canadian, and had only been tempted to enlist by the bounty, selected a seat by the door of the car. I had noticed for some time that he looked nervous and restless, as if he had something on his mind.

At one of our stopping-places, — a small, obscure station, — he crept out of the door, and, as he thought unobserved, dodged behind a shed, thinking, no doubt, that the train would go off without him. But an officer had his eye upon him, and a minute afterwards he was ignominiously brought back and put under guard. I, am glad to say that his case inspired no sympathy. To enlist, obtain a bounty, and then attempt to evade the service for which the bounty is given, is despicable in the extreme. I am glad to know that no others of our company had the least desire to follow this man's example.   .

We passed through New York, Philadelphia, and Washington, but I can give you little idea of either of these cities. The time we passed in each was mostly during the hours of darkness, when there was little opportunity of seeing anything.

In Washington, I was fortunate enough to see our worthy President. We were marching down Pennsylvania Avenue at the time. On the opposite side of the street we descried a very tall man, of slender figure, walking thoughtfully along, not appearing to notice what was passing around him.

The officer in command turned and said : " Boys, look sharp. That is Abraham Lincoln, across the way."

Of course we all looked eagerly towards the man of whom we had heard so much.

I could not help thinking how great a responsibility rests upon this man, — to how great an extent the welfare and destinies of our beloved country depend upon his patriotic course.

As I noticed his features, which, plain as they are, bear the unmistakable marks of a shrewd benevo-

XVI.

FRANK MAKES A FRIEND.

HENRY MORTON rose with the sun. This was not so early as may be supposed, for already November had touched its middle point, and the tardy sun did not make its appearance till nearly seven o'clock. As he passed through the hall he noticed that breakfast was not quite ready.

"A little walk will sharpen my appetite," he thought.

He put on his hat, and passing through the stable-yard at the rear, climbed over a fence and ascended a hill which he had observed from his chamber-window. The sloping sides, which had not yet wholly lost their appearance of verdure, were dotted with trees, mostly apple-trees.

"It must be delightful in summer," said the young man, as he looked thoughtfully about him.

The hill was by no means high, and five minutes walk brought him to the summit. From this spot he had a fine view of the village which lay at his feet embowered in trees. A narrow river wound like a silver thread through the landscape. Groups of trees on either bank bent over as if to see themselves

reflected in the rapid stream. At one point a dam
had been built across from bank to bank, above which
the river widened and deepened, affording an excellent skating-ground for the boys in the cold days of
December and January. A whirring noise was
heard. The grist-mill had just commenced its work
for the day. Down below the dam the shallow
water eddied and whirled, breaking in fleecy foam
over protuberant rocks which lay in the river-bed.

The old village church with its modest proportions
occupied a knoll between the hill and the river. It
was girdled about with firs intermingled with elms.
Near by was a small triangular common, thickly planted with trees, each facing a separate street. Houses
clustered here and there. Comfortable buildings
they were, but built evidently rather for use than
show. The architect had not yet come to the assistance of the village carpenter.

Seen in the cheering light of the rising sun, Henry
Morton could not help feeling that a beautiful picture
was spread out before him.

"After all," he said, thoughtfully, "we need n't
go abroad for beauty, when we can find so much of
it at our own doors. Yet, perhaps the more we see
of the beautiful, the better we are fitted to appreciate
it in the wonderful variety of its numberless forms."

He slowly descended the hill, but in a different direction. This brought him to the road that connected the village with North Rossville, two miles distant.

Coming from a different direction, a boy reached the stile about the same time with himself, and both clambered over together.

"It is a beautiful morning," said the young man, courteously.

"Yes, sir," was the respectful answer. "Have you been up looking at the view?"

"Yes, — and to get an appetite for breakfast. And you?"

Frank Frost (for it was he) laughed. "O, I am here on quite a different errand," he said. "I used to come here earlier in the season to drive the cows to pasture. I come this morning to carry some milk to a neighbor who takes it of us. She usually sends for it, but her son is just now sick with the measles."

"Yet I think you cannot fail to enjoy the pleasant morning, even if you are here for other purposes."

"I do enjoy it very much," said Frank. "When I read of beautiful scenery in other countries, I always wish that I could visit them, and see for myself."

"Perhaps you will some day."

Frank smiled, and shook his head incredulously. "I am afraid there is not much chance of it," he said.

"So I thought when I was of your age," returned Henry Morton.

"Then you have travelled?" said Frank, looking interested.

" Yes.   I have visited most of the countries of Europe."

" Have you been in Rome?" inquired Frank.

" Yes.   Are you interested in Rome?"

" Who could help it, sir?   I should like to see the Capitol, and the Via Sacra, and the Tarpeian Rock, and the Forum,— and, in fact, Rome must be full of objects of interest.   Who knows but I might tread where Cicero, and Virgil, and Cæsar had trodden before me?"

Henry Morton looked at the boy who stood beside him with increased interest.   " I see you are quite a scholar," he said.   " Where did you learn about all these men and places?"

" I have partly prepared for college," answered Frank; " but my father went to the war some weeks since, and I am staying at home to take charge of the farm, and supply his place as well as I can."

" It must have been quite a sacrifice to you to give up your studies?" said his companion.

" Yes, sir, it was a great sacrifice; but we must all of us sacrifice something in these times.   Even the boys can do something for their country."

" What is your name?" asked Henry Morton, more and more pleased with his chance acquaintance. " I should like to become better acquainted with you."

Frank blushed, and his expressive face showed that he was gratified by the compliment.

"My name is Frank Frost," he answered, "and I live about half a mile from here."

"And I am Henry Morton. I am stopping temporarily at the hotel. Shall you be at leisure this evening, Frank?"

"Yes, sir."

"Then I should be glad to receive a call from you. I have no acquaintances, and perhaps we may help each other to make the evening pass pleasantly. I have some pictures collected abroad, which I think you might like to look at."

"I shall be delighted to come," said Frank, his eyes sparkling with pleasure.

By this time they had reached the church, which was distant but a few rods from the hotel. They had just turned the corner of the road, when the clang of a bell was heard.

"I suppose that is my breakfast-bell," said the young man. "It finds me with a good appetite. Good-morning, Frank. I will expect you, then, this evening."

Frank returned home, feeling quite pleased with his invitation.

"I wish," thought he, "that I might see considerable of Mr. Morton. I could learn a great deal from him, he has seen so much."

His road led him past the house of Squire Haynes. John was sauntering about the yard with his hands in his pockets.

12

"Good-morning, John," said Frank, in a pleasant voice.

John did not seem inclined to respond to this politeness. On seeing Frank he scowled, and without deigning to make a reply turned his back and went into the house. He had not forgotten the last occasion on which they had met in the woods, when Frank defeated his cruel designs upon poor Pomp. There was not much likelihood that he would forget it very soon.

"I can't understand John," thought Frank. "The other boys will get mad and get over it before the next day; John broods over it for weeks. I really believe he hates me. But of course I couldn't act any differently. I wasn't going to stand by and see Pomp beaten. I should do just the same again."

The day wore away, and in the evening Frank presented himself at the hotel, and inquired for Mr. Morton. He was ushered up stairs, and told to knock at the door of a room in the second story.

His knock was answered by the young man in person, who shook his hand with a pleasant smile, and invited him in.

"I am glad to see you, Frank," he said, very cordially.

"And I am much obliged to you for inviting me, Mr. Morton."

They sat down together beside the table, and con-

versed on a variety of topics. Frank had numberless questions to ask about foreign scenes and countries, all of which were answered with the utmost
readiness. Henry Morton brought out a large port-
folio containing various pictures, some on note paper,
representing scenes in different parts of Europe.

The evening wore away only too rapidly for Frank.
He had seldom passed two hours so pleasantly. At
half past nine, he rose, and said half regretfully, " I
wish you were going to live in the village this winter,
Mr. Morton."

The young man smiled. " Such is my intention,
Frank," he said, quietly.

" Shall you stay?" said Frank, joyfully. " I suppose you will board here."

" I should prefer a quieter boarding-place. Can
you recommend one?"

Frank hesitated.

" Where," continued Mr. Morton, " I could enjoy the companionship of an intelligent young gentleman of your age?"

" If we lived nearer the village," Frank began,
and stopped abruptly.

" Half a mile would be no objection to me. As I
don't think you will find it unpleasant, Frank, I will
authorize you to offer your mother five dollars a
week for a room and a seat at her table."

" I am quite sure she would be willing, Mr.
Morton, but I am afraid we should not live well

enough to suit you. And I don't think you ought to pay so much as five dollars a week."

"Leave that to me, Frank. My main object is to obtain a pleasant home; and that I am sure I should find at your house."

"Thank you, sir," said Frank; "I will mention it to my mother, and let you know in the course of to-morrow."

XVII.

A SHADE OF MYSTERY.

FRANK found little difficulty in persuading his mother to accept young Morton's proposition. From her son's description she felt little doubt that he would be a pleasant addition to the family circle, while his fund of information would make him instructive as well as agreeable.

There was another consideration besides which determined her to take him. Five dollars a week would go a great ways in housekeeping, or rather, as their income from other sources would probably be sufficient for this, she could lay aside the entire amount towards paying the mortgage held by Squire Haynes. This plan occurred simultaneously to Frank and his mother.

"I should certainly feel myself to blame if I neglected so good an opportunity of helping your father," said Mrs. Frost.

"Suppose we don't tell him, mother," suggested Frank; "but when he gets home surprise him with the amount of our savings."

"No," said Mrs. Frost, after a moment's thought, "your father will be all the better for all the good

12*

news we can send him.   It will make his life more
tolerable."

Frank harnessed his horse to a light wagon and
drove down to the tavern.

Henry Morton was sitting on the piazza, as the
day was unusually warm, with a book in his hand.

" Well," he said, looking up with a smile, " I
hope you have come for me."

" That is my errand, Mr. Morton," answered
Frank.   " If your trunk is already packed, we will
take it along with us."

" It is quite ready.   If you will come up and help
me down stairs with it, I will settle with the land-
lord and leave at once."

This was speedily arranged, and the young man
soon occupied a seat beside Frank.

· Arrived at the farm-house, Frank introduced the
new boarder to his mother.

" I hope we shall be able to make you comfort··
able," said Mrs. Frost, in a hospitable tone.

" I entertain no doubt of it," he said, politely.
" I am easy to suit, and I foresee that Frank and I
will become intimate friends."

" He was very urgent to have you come.   I am
not quite sure whether it would have been safe for
me to refuse."

" I hope he will be as urgent to have me stay.
That will be a still higher compliment."

" Here is the room you are to occupy, Mr. Morton," said Mrs. Frost, opening a door at the head of the front stairs.

It was a large square room, occupying the front eastern corner of the house. The furniture was neat and comfortable, though not pretentious.

"I like this," said the young man, surveying his new quarters with an air of satisfaction. "The sun will find me out in the morning."

"Yes, it will remain with you through the forenoon. I think you will find the room warm and comfortable. But whenever you get tired of it you will be welcome down stairs."

"That is an invitation of which I shall be only too glad to avail myself. Now, Frank, if you will be kind enough to help me up stairs with my trunk."

The trunk was carried up between them, and placed in a closet.

"I will send for a variety of articles from the city to make my room look social and cheerful," said Mr. Morton. "I have some books and engravings in Boston, which I think will contribute to make it so."

A day or two later, two large boxes arrived, one containing pictures, the other books. Of the latter there were perhaps a hundred and fifty, choice and well selected.

Frank looked at them with avidity.

"You shall be welcome to use them as freely as you like," said their owner, — an offer which Frank gratefully accepted.

The engravings were tastefully framed in black wal-
nut. One represented one of Raphael's Madonnas.
Another was a fine photograph, representing a pal-
ace in Venice. · Several others portrayed foreign
scenes. Among them was a street scene in Rome.
An entire family were sitting in different postures on
the portico of a fine building, the man with his
swarthy features half concealed under a slouched hat,
the woman holding a child in her lap, while another,
a boy with large black eyes, leaned his head upon
her knees.

"That represents a Roman family at home," explained Henry Morton.

"At home!"

"Yes, it is the only home they have. They sleep
wherever night finds them, sheltering themselves from
the weather as well as they can."

"But how do they get through the winter? I
should think they would freeze."

"Nature has bestowed upon Italy a mild climate,
so that although they may find the exposure at this
season disagreeable, they are in no danger of freezing."

There was another engraving which Frank looked
at curiously. It represented a wagon laden with
casks of wine, and drawn by an ox and a donkey
yoked together. Underneath was a descriptive phrase,
" Carro di vino."

"You don't see such teams in this country," said
Mr. Morton, smiling. "In Italy they are common

enough. In the background you notice a priest with a shovel-hat, sitting sideways on a donkey. Such a sight is much more common there than that of a man on horseback. Indeed, this stubborn animal is found very useful in ascending and descending mountains, being much surer-footed than the horse. I have ridden down steep descents along the verge of a precipice where it would have been madness to venture on horseback, but I felt the strongest confidence in the donkey I bestrode."

Frank noticed a few Latin books in the collection. "Do you read Latin, Mr. Morton?" he inquired.

"Yes, with tolerable ease. If I can be of any assistance to you in carrying on your Latin studies, it will afford me pleasure to do so."

"I am very much obliged to you, Mr. Morton. I tried to go on with it by myself, but every now and then I came to a difficult sentence which I could not make out."

"I think we can overcome the difficulties between us. At any rate we will try. Have no hesitation in applying to me."

Before closing this chapter, I think it necessary to narrate a little incident which served to heighten the interest with which Frank regarded his new friend, though it involved the latter in a shadow of mystery.

Mrs. Frost did not keep what in New England is denominated "help." Being in good health, she performed the greater part of her household tasks unassisted. When washing and house-cleaning days came, however, she obtained outside assistance. For this purpose she engaged Chloe to come twice a week, on Monday and Saturday, not only because in this way she could help the woman to earn a living, but also because she found her a valuable and efficient assistant.

Henry Morton became a member of the little household at the farm on Thursday, and two days later Chloe came as usual to " clean house."

The young man was standing in the front yard as Chloe, with a white turban on her head, for she had not yet laid aside her Southern mode of dress, came from the street by a little path which led to the back door. Her attention was naturally drawn to the young man. No sooner did she obtain a full view of him, than she stopped short and exclaimed with every appearance of surprise, " Why, Mass' Richard, who 'd a thought to see you here. You look just like you used to, dat's a fac. It does my old eyes good to see you."

Henry Morton turned suddenly.

" What, Chloe ! " he exclaimed in equal surprise. " What brings you up here?—I thought you were miles away in Virginia."

" So I was, Mass' Richard. But lor' bless you, when de Linkum sogers come, I could n't stay no longer. I took and runned away."

" And here you are, then."

" Yes, Mass' Richard, here I is, for sure."

" How do you like the North, Chloe ? "

" Don't like it as well as de Souf. It's too cold,"
and Chloe shivered.

" But you would rather be here than there ? "

" Yes, Mass' Richard. Here I own myself.
Don't have no oberseer to crack his whip at me now.
I 'se a free woman now, and so 's my little Pomp."

The young man smiled at the innocent mistake.

" Pomp is your little boy, I suppose, Chloe."

" Yes, Mass' Richard."

" Is he a good boy ? "

" He's as sassy as de debbel," said Chloe, emphatically. " I don't know what 's going to come of dat
boy. He 's most worried my life out."

" O, he 'll grow better as he grows older. — Don't
trouble yourself about him. But, Chloe, there 's
one favor I am going to ask of you."

" Yes, Mass' Richard."

" Don't call me by my real name. For some
reasons, which I can't at present explain, I prefer to
be known as Henry Morton, for some months to come.
Do you think you can remember to call me by that
name ? "

" Yes, Mass' — Henry," said Chloe, looking perplexed.

Henry Morton turned round to meet the surprised
looks of Frank and his mother.

" My friends," he said, " I hope you will not feel

distrustful of me, when I freely acknowledge to you
that imperative reasons compel me for a time to appear under a name not my own.   Chloe and I are
old acquaintances, but I must request her to keep
secret for a time her past knowledge concerning me.
I think," he added with a smile, " that she would
have nothing to say that would damage me.   Some
time you shall know all.   Are you satisfied ? "

" Quite so," said Mrs. Frost.   " I have no doubt
you have good and sufficient reasons."

" I will endeavor to justify your confidence," said
Henry Morton, an expression of pleasure lighting up
his face.

XVIII.

THANKSGIVING AT THE FARM.

THE chill November days drew to a close. The shrill winds whistled through the branches of the trees, and stirred the leaves which lay in brown heaps upon the ground. But at the end of the month came Thanksgiving, — the farmer's Harvest Home. The fruits of the field were in abundance, but in many a home there were vacant chairs, never more, alas! to be filled. But he who dies in a noble cause leaves sweet and fragrant memories behind, which shall ever after make it pleasant to think of him.

Thanksgiving morning dawned foggy and cold. Yet there is something in the name that warms the heart and makes the dullest day seem bright. The sunshine of the heart more than compensates for the absence of sunshine without.

Frank had not been idle.

The night before he helped Jacob kill a Turkey and a pair of chickens, and seated on a box in the barn they had picked them clean in preparation for the morrow.

Within the house too, might be heard the notes of busy preparation. Alice, sitting in a low chair,

was busily engaged in chopping meat for mince-pies.
Maggie sat near her paring pumpkins, for a genuine
New England Thanksgiving cannot be properly cele-
brated without pumpkin pies. Even little Charlie
found work to do in slicing apples.

By evening a long row of pies might be seen upon
the kitchen dresser. Brown and flaky they looked,
fit for the table of a prince. So the children thought
as they surveyed the attractive array, and felt that
Thanksgiving, come as often as it might, could never
be unwelcome.

Through the forenoon of Thanksgiving Day the
preparations continued. Frank and Mr. Morton
went to the village church, where an appropriate
service was held by Rev. Mr. Apthorp. There were
but few of the village matrons present. They were
mostly detained at home by housewifely cares, which
on that day could not well be delegated to other
hands.

"Mr. Morton," said Frank, as they walked
leisurely home, "did you notice how Squire Haynes
stared at you this morning?"

Mr. Morton looked interested. "Did he?" he
asked. "I did not notice."

"Yes, he turned half round, and looked at you
with a puzzled expression, as if he thought he had
seen you somewhere before, but could not recall who
you were."

"Perhaps I reminded him of some one he has

known in past years," said the young man, quietly. "We sometimes find strange resemblances in utter strangers."

"I think he must have felt quite interested," pursued Frank, "for he stopped me after church, and inquired who you were."

"Indeed!" said Henry Morton, quietly. "And what did you tell him?"

"I told him your name, and mentioned that you were boarding with us."

"What then? Did he make any further inquiries?"

"He asked where you came from."

"He seemed quite curious about me. I ought to feel flattered. And what did you reply?"

"I told him I did not know, — that I only knew that part of your life had been passed in Europe. I heard him say under his breath, ' it is singular.'"

"Frank," said Mr. Morton, after a moment's thought, "I wish to have Squire Haynes learn as little of me as possible. If, therefore, he should ask you how I am employed, you may say that I have come here for the benefit of my health. This is one of my motives, though not the principal one."

"I will remember," said Frank. "I don't think he will say much to me, however. He has a grudge against father, and his son does not like me. I am sorry that father is compelled to have some business relations with the Squire."

" Indeed ! "

" Yes, he holds a mortgage on our farm for eight hundred dollars. It was originally more, but it has been reduced to this. He will have the right to foreclose on the first of July."

" Shall you have the money ready for him at that time."

" No ; we may have half enough, perhaps. I am sometimes troubled when I think of it. Father feels confident, however, that the Squire will not be hard upon us, but will renew the mortgage."

Henry Morton looked very thoughtful, but said nothing.

They had now reached the farm-house.

Dinner was already on the table. In the centre, on a large dish, was the turkey, done to a turn. It was flanked by the chickens on a smaller dish. These were supported by various vegetables, such as the season supplied. A dish of cranberry sauce stood at one end of the table, and at the opposite end a dish of apple sauce.

" Do you think you can carve the turkey, Mr. Morton ? " asked Mrs. Frost.

" I will at least make the attempt."

" I want the wish-bone, Mr. Morton," said Maggie.

" No, I want it," said Charlie.

" You shall both have one," said the mother. Luckily each of the chickens is provided with one."

"I know what I am going to wish," said Charlie, nodding his head with decision.

"Well, Charlie, what is it?" asked Frank.

"I shall wish that papa may come home safe."

"And so will I," said Maggie.

"I wish he might sit down with us to-day," said Mrs. Frost with a little sigh. "He has never before been absent from us on Thanksgiving Day."

"Was he well when you last heard from him?"

"Yes, but hourly expecting orders to march to join the army in Maryland. I am afraid he won't get as good a Thanksgiving dinner as this."

"Two years ago," said Mr. Morton, I ate my Thanksgiving dinner in Amsterdam."

"Do they have Thanksgiving there, Mr. Morton?" inquired Alice.

"No, they know nothing of our good New England festival. I was obliged to order a special dinner for myself. I don't think you would have recognized plum pudding under the name which they gave it."

"What was it?" asked Frank, curiously.

"*Blom buden* was the name given on the bill."

"I can spell better than that," said Charlie.

"We shall have to send you out among the Dutchmen as a schoolmaster plenipotentiary," said Frank, laughing. "I hope the 'blom buden' was good in spite of the way it was spelt."

"Yes, it was very good."

13*

"I don't believe it beat mother's," said Charlie.

"At your present rate of progress, Charlie, you won't leave room for any," said Frank.

"I wish I had two stomachs," said Charlie, looking regretfully at the inviting delicacies which tempted him with what the French call the embarrassment of riches.

"Well done, Charlie!" laughed his mother.

Dinner was at length over. Havoc and desolation reigned upon the once well-filled table.

In the evening, as they all sat together round the table, Maggie climbed on Mr. Morton's knee and petitioned for a story.

"What shall it be about?" he asked.

"O, anything."

"Let me think a moment," said the young man.

He bent his eyes thoughtfully upon the wood fire that crackled in the wide open fireplace, and soon signified that he was ready to begin.

All the children gathered around him, and even Mrs. Frost, sitting quietly at her knitting, edged her chair a little nearer, that she too might listen to Mr. Morton's story. As this was of some length, we shall devote to it a separate chapter.

XIX.

THE WONDERFUL TRANSFORMATION.

" My story," commenced Mr. Morton, " is rather a remarkable one in some respects; and I cannot vouch for its being true. I shall call it ' The Wonderful Transformation.'

" Thomas Tubbs was a prosperous little tailor, and for forty years had been a resident of the town of Webbington, where he had been born and brought up. I have called him little, and you will agree with me when I say that, even in high-heeled boots, which he always wore, he measured only four feet and a half in height.

" In spite, however, of his under-size, Thomas had succeeded in winning the hand of a woman fifteen inches taller than himself. If this extra height had been divided equally between them, possibly they might have attracted less observation. As it was, when they walked to church, the top of the little tailor's beaver just about reached the shoulders of Mrs. Tubbs. Nevertheless, they managed to live very happily together, for the most part, though now and then, when Thomas was a little refractory, his better half would snatch him up bodily, and, carrying him to the cellar, lock him up there. Such little incidents only served to spice their domestic life, and were usually followed by a warm reconciliation.

"The happy pair had six children, all of whom took after their mother, and promised to be tall; the oldest boy, twelve years of age, being already taller than his father, or rather he would have been but for the tall hat and high-heeled boots.

"Mr. Tubbs was a tailor, as I have said. One day there came into his shop a man attired with extreme shabbiness. Thomas eyed him askance.

"'Mr. Tubbs,' said the stranger, 'as you perceive, I am out at elbows. I would like to get you to make me up a suit of clothes.'

"'Ahem!' coughed Thomas, and glanced upwards at a notice affixed to the door, 'Terms, Cash.'

"The stranger's eye followed the direction of Mr. Tubbs's. He smiled.

"'I frankly confess,' he said, 'that I shall not be able to pay immediately, but, if I live, I will pay you within six months.'

"'How am I to feel sure of that?' asked the tailor, hesitating.

"'I pledge my word,' was the reply. 'You see, Mr. Tubbs, I have been sick for some time past, and that, of course, has used up my money. Now, thank Providence, I am well again, and ready to go to work. But I need clothes, as you see, before I have the ability to pay for them.'

" ' What's your name ?' asked Thomas.

" ' Oswald Rudenheimer,' was the reply.

" ' A foreigner?'

" ' As you may suppose. Now, Mr. Tubbs, what do you say? Do you think you can trust me?'

" Thomas examined the face of his visitor. He looked honest, and the little tailor had a good deal of confidence in the excellence of human nature.

" ' I may be foolish,' he said at last, ' but I'll do it.'

" ' A thousand thanks !' said the stranger. ' You shan't repent of it.'

" The cloth was selected, and Thomas set to work. In three days the suit was finished, and Thomas sat in his shop waiting for his customer. At last he came, but what a change ! He was splendidly dressed. The little tailor hardly recognized him.

" ' Mr. Tubbs,' said he, ' you're an honest man and a good fellow. You trusted me when I appeared penniless, but I deceived you. I am really one of the genii, of whom perhaps you have read, and lineally descended from those who guarded Solomon's seal. Instead of making you wait for your pay, I will recompense you on the spot, either in money or —— '

" ' Or what?' asked the astonished tailor.

" ' Or I will grant the first wish that may be formed in your mind. Now choose.'

" Thomas did not take long to choose. His charge

would amount to but a few dollars, while he might
wish for a million. He signified his decision.

" ' Perhaps you have chosen wisely," said his visitor. ' But mind that you are careful about your
wish. You may wish for something you don't want.'

" ' No fear of that,' said the tailor, cheerfully.

" ' At any rate, I will come this way six months
hence, and should you then wish to be released from
the consequences of your wish, and to receive instead
the money stipulated as the price of the suit, I will
give you the chance.'

" Of course Thomas did not object, though he
considered it rather a foolish provision.

" His visitor disappeared, and the tailor was left
alone. He laid aside his work. How could a man
be expected to work who had only to wish, and he
could come into possession of more than he could
earn in a hundred or even a thousand years?

" ' I might as well enjoy myself a little,' thought
Mr. Tubbs. ' Let me see. I think there is a show
in the village to-day. I'll go to it.'

" He accordingly slipped on his hat and went out,
somewhat to the surprise of his wife, who concluded
that her husband must be going out on business.

" Thomas Tubbs wended his way to the market-
place. He pressed in among the people, a crowd of
whom had already assembled to witness the show.
I cannot tell you what the show was. I am only
concerned in telling you what Thomas Tubbs saw

and did; and, to tell the plain truth, he did n't see anything at all. He was wedged in among people a foot or two taller than himself. Now it is not pleasant to hear all about you laughing heartily and not even catch a glimpse of what amuses them so much. Thomas Tubbs was human, and as curious as most people. Just as a six-footer squeezed in front of him he could not help framing, in his vexations, this wish, —

" ' O dear! I wish I were ten feet high!'

" Luckless Thomas Tubbs! Never had he framed a more unfortunate wish. On the instant he shot up from an altitude of four feet six to ten feet. Fortunately his clothes expanded proportionally. So, instead of being below the medium height, he was raised more than four feet above it.

" Of course his immediate neighbors became aware of the gigantic presence, though they did not at all recognize its identity with the little tailor, Thomas Tubbs.

" At once there was a shout of terror. The crowd scattered in all directions, forgetting the spectacle at which, the moment before, they had been laughing heartily, and the little tailor, no longer little, was left alone in the market-place.

" ' Good heavens!' he exclaimed in bewilderment, stretching out his brawny arm, nearly five feet in length, and staring at it in ludicrous astonishment, ' who 'd have thought that I should ever be so tall?'

" To tell the truth, the little man — I mean Mr. Tubbs — at first rather enjoyed his new magnitude. He had experienced mortification so long on account of his diminutive stature, that he felt a little exhilarated at the idea of being able to look down on those to whom he had hitherto felt compelled to look up. It was rather awkward to have people afraid of him. As he turned to leave the Square, for the exhibitor of the show had run off in the general panic, he could see people looking at him from third-story windows, and pointing at him with outstretched fingers and mouths agape.

" ' Really,' thought Thomas Tubbs, ' I never expected to be such an object of interest. I think I'll go home.'

" His house was a mile off, but so large were his strides that five minutes carried him to it.

" Now Mrs. Tubbs was busy putting the dinner on the table, and wondering why her husband did not make his appearance. She was fully determined to give him a scolding in case his delay was so great as to cause the dinner to cool. All at once she heard a bustle at the door. Looking into the entry, she saw a huge man endeavoring to make his entrance into the house. As the portal was only seven feet in height, it was not accomplished without a great deal of twisting and squirming.

" Mrs. Tubbs turned pale.

" ' What are you trying to do, you monster?' she faltered.

" 'I have come home to dinner, Mary,' was the meek reply.

" '*Come home to dinner!*' exclaimed Mrs. Tubbs, aghast. 'Who in the name of wonder are you, you overgrown brute?'

" 'Who am I?' asked the giant, smiling feebly, for he began to feel a little queer at this reception from the wife with whom he had lived for fifteen years. 'Ha, ha! don't you know your own husband — your Tommy?'

" 'My husband!' exclaimed Mrs. Tubbs, astonished at the fellow's impudence. 'You don't mean to say that you are my husband?'

" 'Of course I am,' said Thomas.

" 'Then,' said Mrs. Tubbs, 'I would have you know that my husband is a respectable little man, not half your size.'

" 'O dear!' thought Thomas. 'Well, here's a kettle of fish; my own wife won't own me!'

" 'So I was,' he said aloud. 'I was only four feet six; but I've — I've grown.'

" 'Grown!' Mrs. Tubbs laughed hysterically. 'That's a likely story, when it's only an hour since my husband went into the street as short as ever. I only wish he'd come in, I do, to expose your imposition.'

" 'But I *have* grown, Mary,' said Tubbs, piteously. 'I was out in the crowd, and I couldn't see what was going on, and so I wished I was ten feet

14

high; and before I knew it I was as tall as I am
now.'

"'No doubt,' said Mrs. Tubbs, incredulously.
'As to that, all I 've got to say is, that you 'd better
wish yourself back again, as I sha n't own you as my
husband till you do!'

"'Really,' thought Mr. Tubbs, 'this is dreadful!
What can I do!'

"Just then one of his children ran into the room.

"'Johnny, come to me,' said his father, implor-
ingly. 'Come to your father.'

"'My father!' said Johnny, shying out of the
room. 'You ain't my father. My father is n't as
tall as a tree.'

"'You see how absurd your claim is,' said Mrs.
Tubbs. 'You 'll oblige me by leaving the house
directly.'

"'Leave the house — my house!' said Tubbs.

"'If you don't, I 'll call in the neighbors,' said
the courageous woman.

"'I don't believe they 'd dare to come,' said
Tubbs, smiling queerly at the recollection of what a
sensation his appearance had made.

"'Won't you go?'

"'At least you 'll let me have some dinner. I
am most famished.'

"'Dinner!' said Mrs. Tubbs, hesitating. 'I
don't think there 's enough in the house. However,
you can sit down to the table.'

" Tubbs attempted to sit down on a chair, but his weight was so great that it was crushed beneath him. Finally, he was compelled to sit on the floor, and even then his stature was such that his head rose to the height of six feet.

" What an enormous appetite he had, too ! The viands on the table seemed nothing. He at first supplied his plate with the usual quantity ; but as the extent of his appetite became revealed to him, he was forced to make way with everything on the table. Even then he was hungry.

" ' Well, I declare,' thought Mrs. Tubbs, in amazement, ' it does take an immense quantity to keep him alive ! '

" Tubbs rose from the table, and in doing so hit his head a smart whack against the ceiling. Before leaving the house he turned to make a last appeal to his wife, who, he could not help seeing, was anxious to have him go.

" ' Won't you own me, Mary ?' he asked. ' It is n't my fault that I am so big.'

" ' Own you !' exclaimed his wife. ' I would n't own you for a mint of money. You 'd eat me out of house and home in less than a week.'

" ' I don't know but I should,' said Mr. Tubbs, mournfully. ' I don't see what gives me such an appetite. I 'm hungry now.'

" ' Hungry, after you 've eaten enough for six !' exclaimed his wife, aghast. ' Well, I never !'

" ' Then you won't let me stay, Mary?

" ' No, no.'

" With slow and sad strides Thomas Tubbs left the house. The world seemed dark enough to the poor fellow. Not only was he disowned by his wife and children, but he could not tell how he should ever earn enough to keep him alive, with the frightful appetite which he now possessed. ' I don't know,' he thought, ' but the best way is to drown myself at once.' So he walked to the river, but found it was not deep enough to drown him.

" As he emerged from the river uncomfortably wet, he saw a man timidly approaching him. It proved to be the manager of the show.

" ' Holloa !' said he, hesitatingly.

" ' Holloa !' returned Tubbs, disconsolately.

" ' Would you like to enter into a business engagement with me ?'

" ' Of what sort?' asked Tubbs, brightening up.

" ' To be exhibited,' was the reply. ' You 're the largest man living in the world. We could make a pretty penny together.'

" Tubbs was glad enough to accept this proposition, which came to him like a plank to a drowning man. Accordingly an agreement was made that, after deducting expenses, he should share profits with the manager.

" It proved to be a great success. From all quarters people flocked to see the great prodigy, the wonder of the world, as he was described in huge posters. Scientific men wrote learned papers in which they strove to explain his extraordinary height, and, as might be expected, no two assigned the same cause.

"At the end of six months Tubbs had five thousand dollars as his share of the profits. But after all he was far from happy. He missed the society of his wife and children, and shed many tears over his separation from them.

"At the end of six months his singular customer again made his appearance.

"'It seems to me you've altered some since I last saw you,' he said, with a smile.

"'Yes,' said Tubbs, dolefully.

"'You don't like the change, I judge?'

"'No,' said Tubbs. 'It separates me from my wife and children, and that makes me unhappy.'

"'Would you like to be changed back again?'

"'Gladly,' was the reply.

"Presto! the wonderful giant was changed back into the little tailor. No sooner was this effected than he returned post-haste to Webbington. His wife received him with open arms.

"'O Thomas,' she exclaimed, 'how could you leave us so? On the day of your disappearance a huge brute of a man came here and pretended to be you, but I soon sent him away.'

"Thomas wisely said nothing, but displayed his five thousand dollars. There was great joy in the little dwelling. Thomas Tubbs at once took a larger shop, and grew every year in wealth and public esteem. The only way in which he did not grow was in stature; but his six months experience as a giant had cured him of any wish of that sort. The last I heard of him was his election to the legislature."

———

"That's a bully story," said Charlie, using a word which he had heard from older boys. "I wish I was a great tall giant."

"What would you do if you were, Charlie?"

"I'd go and fight the Rebels," said Charlie, manfully.

XX.

In the season of leisure from farm work which followed, Frank found considerable time for study. The kind sympathy and ready assistance given by Mr. Morton, made his task a very agreeable one, and his progress for a time was as rapid as if he had remained at school.

He also assumed the office of teacher, having undertaken to give a little elementary instruction to Pomp. Here his task was beset with difficulties. Pomp was naturally bright, but incorrigibly idle. His activity was all misdirected and led him into a wide variety of mischief. He would have been sent to school, but his mischievous propensities had so infected the boys sitting near him, that the teacher had been compelled to request his removal.

Three times in the week, during the afternoon, Pomp came over to the farm for instruction. On the first of these occasions we will look in upon him and his teacher.

Pomp is sitting on a cricket by the kitchen fire. He has a primer open before him at the alphabet. His round eyes are fixed upon the page as long as

Frank is looking at him, but he requires constant watching. His teacher sits near by, with a Latin dictionary resting upon a light stand before him, and a copy of Virgil's Æneid in his hand.

"Well, Pomp, do you think you know your lesson?" he asks.

"Dunno, Mass' Frank; I reckon so."

"You may bring your book to me, and I will try you."

Pomp rose from his stool and sidled up to Frank with no great alacrity.

"What's that letter, Pomp?" asked the young teacher, pointing out the initial letter of the alphabet.

Pomp answered correctly.

"And what is the next!"

Pomp shifted from one foot to the other, and stared vacantly out of the window, but said nothing.

"Don't you know?"

"Pears like I don't member him, Mass' Frank."

Here Frank had recourse to a system of mnemonics frequently resorted to by teachers in their extremity.

"What's the name of the little insect that stings people sometimes, Pomp?"

"Wasp, Mass' Frank," was the confident reply.

"No, I don't mean that. I mean the bee."

"Yes, Mass' Frank."

"Well, this is B."

Pomp looked at it attentively, and after a pause inquired, "Where's him wings, Mass' Frank?"

Frank bit his lips to keep from laughing. "I don't mean that this is a bee that makes honey," he explained, "only it has the same name. Now do you think you can remember how it is called?"

"Bumblebee!" repeated Pomp, triumphantly.

Pomp's error was corrected, and the lesson proceeded.

"What is the next letter?" asked Frank, indicating it with the point of his knife-blade.

"X," answered the pupil, readily.

"No, Pomp," was the dismayed reply. "It is very different from X."

"Dat's him name at school," said Pomp, positively.

"No Pomp, you are mistaken. That is X, away down there."

"Perhaps him change his name," suggested Pomp.

"No. The letters never change their names. I don't think you know your lesson, Pomp. Just listen to me while I tell you the names of some of the letters, and try to remember them."

When this was done, Pomp was directed to sit down on the cricket, and study his lesson for twenty minutes, at the end of which he might again recite.

Pomp sat down, and for five entire minutes seemed absorbed in his book. Then, unfortunately, the cat walked into the room, and soon attracted the attention of the young student. He sidled from his seat so silently that Frank did not hear him. He was soon made sensible that Pomp was engaged in some mischief by hearing a prolonged wail of anguish from the cat.

Looking up, he found that his promising pupil had tied her by the leg to a chair, and under these circumstances was amusing himself by pinching her tail.

"What are you doing there, Pomp?" he asked, quickly.

Pomp scuttled back to his seat, and appeared to be deeply intent upon his primer.

"Ain't doin' noffin', Mass' Frank," he answered, innocently.

"Then how came the cat tied to that chair?"

"'Spec' she must have tied herself."

"Come, Pomp, you know better than that. You know cats can't tie themselves. Get up immediately and unfasten her."

Pomp rose with alacrity, and undertook to release puss from the thraldom of which she had become very impatient. Perhaps she would have been quite as well off if she had been left to herself. The process of liberation did not appear to be very agreeable, judging from the angry mews which proceeded from her. Finally, in her indignation against Pomp for some aggressive act, she scratched him sharply.

"You wicked old debble!" exclaimed Pomp, wrathfully.

He kicked at the cat; but she was lucky enough to escape, and ran out of the room as fast as her four legs could carry her.

" Big ugly debble ! " muttered Pomp, watching the blood ooze from his finger.

" What 's the matter, Pomp ? "

" Old cat scratched me."

" And what did you do to her, Pomp? I am afraid you deserved your scratch."

" Did n't do noffin', Mass' Frank," said Pomp, virtuously.

" I don't think you always tell the truth, Pomp."

" Can't help it, Mass' Frank, 'Spec' I've got a little debble inside of me."

" What do you mean, Pomp! What put that idea in your head ? "

" Dat 's what mammy says. Dat 's what she al'ays tells me."

" Then," said Frank, " I think it will be best to whip it out of you. Where 's my stick ? "

" O no, Mass' Frank," said Pomp, in alarm; " I 'll be good, for sure."

" Then sit down and get your lesson."

Again Pomp assumed his cricket. Before he had time to devise any new mischief, Mrs. Frost came to the head of the stairs and called Frank.

Frank laid aside his books, and presented himself at the foot of the stairs.

" I should like your help a few minutes. Can you leave your studies ? "

" Certainly, mother."

Before going up, he cautioned Pomp to study

quietly, and not get into any mischief, while he was gone. Pomp promised very readily.

Frank had hardly got up stairs before his pupil rose from the cricket, and began to look attentively about him. His first proceeding was to hide his primer carefully in Mrs. Frost's work-basket, which lay on the table. Then, looking curiously about him, his attention was drawn to the old-fashioned clock that stood in the corner.

Now, Pomp's curiosity had been strongly excited by this clock. It was not quite clear to him how the striking part was effected. Here seemed to be a favorable opportunity for instituting an investigation. Pomp drew his cricket to the clock, and opening it tried to reach up to the face. But he was not yet high enough. He tried a chair, and still required a greater elevation. Espying Frank's Latin dictionary, he pressed that into the service.

By and by Frank and his mother heard the clock striking an unusual number of times.

"What is the matter with the clock?" inquired Mrs. Frost.

"I don't know," said Frank, unsuspiciously.

"It has struck ten times, and it is only four o'clock."

"I wonder if Pomp can have got at it," said Frank, with a sudden thought.

He ran down stairs hastily.

Pomp heard him coming, and in his anxiety to

escape detection, contrived to lose his balance and fall to the floor. As he fell, he struck the table, on which a pan of sour milk had been placed, and it was overturned, deluging poor Pomp with the unsavory fluid.

Pomp shrieked and kicked most energetically. His appearance, as he picked himself up, was ludicrous in the extreme. His sable face was plentifully besprinkled with clotted milk, giving him the appearance of a negro who is coming out white in spots. The floor was swimming in milk. Luckily the dictionary had fallen clear of it, and so escaped.

"Is this the way you study?" demanded Frank, as sternly as his sense of the ludicrous plight in which he found Pomp would permit.

For once Pomp's ready wit deserted him. He had nothing to say.

"Go out and wash yourself."

Pomp came back rather shamefaced, his face restored to its original color.

"Now, where is your book?"

Pomp looked about him, but, as he took good care not to look where he knew his book to be, of course he did not find it.

"I 'clare, Mass' Frank, it done lost," he at length asserted.

"How can it be lost when you had it only a few minutes ago?"

"I dunno," answered Pomp, stolidly.

15

" Have you been out of the room?"

Pomp answered in the negative.

" Then it must be somewhere here."

Frank went quietly to the corner of the room and took therefrom a stick.

" Now, Pomp," he said, " I will give you just two minutes to find the book in. If you don't find it, I shall have to give you a whipping."

Pomp looked at his teacher to see if he was in earnest. Seeing that he was, he judged it best to find the book.

Looking into the work-box, he said, innocently, " I 'clare to gracious, Mass' Frank, if it has n't slipped down yere. Dat's mi'ty cur's, dat is."

" Pomp, sit down," said Frank, " I am going to talk to you seriously. What makes you tell so many lies?"

" Dunno any better," replied Pomp, grinning.

" Yes, you do, Pomp. Does n't your mother tell you not to lie?"

" Lor', Mass' Frank, she's poor ignorant nigger. She don't know noffin'."

" You must n't speak so of your mother. She brings you up as well as she knows how. She has to work hard for you, and you ought to love her."

" So I do, 'cept when she licks me."

" If you behave properly she won't whip you. You'll grow up a ' poor ignorant nigger ' yourself if you don't study."

" Shall I get white, Mass' Frank, if I study?" asked Pomp, showing a double row of white teeth.

" You were white enough just now," said Frank, smiling.

" Yah, yah!" returned Pomp, who appreciated the joke.

" Now, Pomp," Frank continued seriously, " if you will learn your lesson in fifteen minutes I will give you a piece of gingerbread."

" I'll do it, Mass' Frank," said Pomp, promptly.

Pomp was very fond of gingerbread, as Frank very well knew. In the time specified the lesson was got, and recited satisfactorily.

As Pomp's education will not again be referred to, it may be said that when Frank had discovered how to manage him, he learned quite rapidly. Chloe, who was herself unable to read, began to look upon Pomp with a new feeling of respect when she found that he could read stories in words of one syllable, and the " lickings " of which he complained became less frequent. But his love of fun still remained, and occasionally got him into trouble, as we shall hereafter have occasion to see.

XXI. ·

THE BATTLE OF FREDERICKSBURG.

ABOUT the middle of December came the sad tragedy of Fredericksburg, in which thousands of our gallant soldiers yielded up their lives in a hard, unequal struggle, which brought forth nothing but mortification and disaster.

The first telegrams which appeared in the daily papers brought anxiety and bodings of ill to many households. The dwellers at the farm were not exempt. They had been apprised by a recent letter that Mr. Frost's regiment now formed a part of the grand army which lay encamped on the eastern side of the Rappahannock. The probability was that he was engaged in the battle. Frank realized for the first time to what peril his father was exposed, and mingled with the natural feeling which such a thought was likely to produce, was the reflection that, but for him, his father would have been in safety at home.

" Did I do right ? " Frank asked himself anxiously, the old doubt recurring once more.

Then, above the selfish thought of peril to him and his, rose the consideration of the country's need, and Frank said to himself, "I have done right, — whatever happens. I feel sure of that."

Yet his anxiety was by no means diminished, especially when, a day or two afterwards, tidings of the great disaster came to hand, only redeemed by the masterly retreat across the river, in which a great army, without the loss of a single gun, ambulance, or wagon, withdrew from the scene of a hopeless struggle, under the very eyes of the enemy, yet escaping discovery.

One afternoon Frank went to the post-office a little after the usual time. As he made his way through a group at the door, he noticed compassionate glances directed towards him.

His heart gave a sudden bound.

"Has anything happened to my father?" he inquired with pale face. "Have any of you heard anything?"

"He is wounded, Frank," said the nearest bystander.

"Show it to me," said Frank.

In the evening paper, which was placed in his hands, he read a single line, but of fearful import; "Henry Frost, wounded." Whether the wound was slight or serious, no intimation was given.

Frank heaved a sigh of comparative relief. His father was not dead, as he at first feared. Yet, he felt that the suspense would be a serious trial. He did not know how to tell his mother. She met him at the gate. His serious face and lagging steps revealed the truth, exciting at first apprehensions of something even more serious.

For two days they remained without news. Then came a letter from the absent father, which wonderfully lightened all their hearts. The fact that he was able to write a long letter with his own hand, showed plainly that his wound must be a trifling one. The letter ran thus : —

DEAR MARY :—

I fear that the report of my wound will reach you before this letter comes to assure you that it is a mere scratch, and scarcely worth a thought. I cannot for an instant think of it, when I consider how many of our poor fellows have been mowed down by instant death, or are now lying with ghastly wounds on pallets in the hospital. We have been through a fearful trial, and the worst thought is that our losses are not compensated by a single advantage.

Before giving you an account of it from the point of view of a private soldier, let me set your mind at rest by saying that my injury is only a slight flesh wound in the arm, which will necessitate my carrying it in a sling for a few days; that is all.

Early on the morning of Thursday, the 10th inst., the first act in the great drama commenced with laying the pontoon bridges over which our men were to make their way into the Rebel city. My own division was to cross directly opposite the city. All honor to the brave men who volunteered to lay the bridges. It was a trying and perilous duty. On the other side, in rifle-pits and houses at the brink of the river, were posted the enemy's sharpshooters, and these at a given signal opened fire upon our poor fellows who were necessarily unprotected. The firing was so severe and deadly, and impossible to escape from, that for the time we were obliged to desist. Before anything could be effected it became clear that the sharpshooters must be dislodged.

Then opened the second scene.

A deluge of shot and shell from our side of the river rained upon the city, setting some buildings on fire, and severely damaging others. It was a most exciting spectacle to us who watched from the bluff, knowing that erelong we must make the perilous passage, and confront the foe, the mysterious silence of whose batteries inspired alarm, as indicating a consciousness of power.

The time of our trial came at length.

Towards the close of the afternoon General Howard's division, to which I belong, crossed the pontoon bridge whose building had cost us more than one gallant soldier. The distance was short, for the Rappahannock at this point is not more than a quarter of a mile wide. In a few minutes we were marching through the streets of Fredericksburg. We gained possession of the lower streets, but not without some street fighting, in which our brigade lost about one hundred in killed and wounded.

For the first time I witnessed violent death. The man marching by my side suddenly reeled, and pressing his hand to his breast fell forward. Only a moment before he had spoken to me, saying, "I think we are going to have hot work." Now he was dead, shot through the heart. I turned sick with horror, but there was no time to pause. We must march on, not knowing that our turn might not come next. Each of us felt that he bore his life in his hand.

But this was soon over, and orders came that we should bivouac for the night. You will not wonder that I lay awake nearly the whole night. A night attack was possible, and the confusion and darkness would have made it fearful. As I lay awake I could not help thinking how anxious you would feel if you had known where I was.

So closed the first day.

The next dawned warm and pleasant. In the quiet of the morning it seemed hard to believe that we were on the eve of a bloody struggle. Discipline was not very strictly maintained. Some of our number left the ranks and ransacked the houses, more from curiosity than the desire to pillage.

I went down to the bank of the river, and took a look at the bridge which it had cost us so much trouble to throw across. It bore frequent marks of the firing of the day previous.

At one place I came across an old negro, whose white head and wrinkled face indicated an advanced age. Clinging to him were two children, of perhaps four and six years of age, who had been crying.

" Don't cry, honey," I heard him say, soothingly, wiping the tears from the cheeks of the youngest with a coarse cotton handkerchief.

" I want mamma," said the child, piteously.

A sad expression came over the old black's face.

" What is the matter?" I asked, advancing towards him.

" She is crying for her mother," he said.

" Is she dead?"

" Yes, sir; she'd been ailing for a long time, and the guns of yesterday hastened her death."

" Where did you live?"

" In that house yonder, sir."

" Did n't you feel afraid when we fired on the town?"

" We were all in the cellar, sir. One shot struck the house, but did not injure it much."

" You use very good language," I could not help saying.

" Yes, sir; I have had more advantages than most of — of my class." These last words he spoke rather bitterly. " When I was a young man my master amused himself with teaching me; but he found I learned so fast that he stopped short. But I carried it on by myself."

" Did n't you find that difficult ? "

" Yes, sir; but my will was strong. I managed to get books, now one way, now another. I have read considerable, sir."

This he said with some pride.

" Have you ever read Shakespeare ? "

" In part, sir; but I never could get hold of Hamlet. I have always wanted to read that play."

I drew him out, and was astonished at the extent of his information, and the intelligent judgments which he expressed.

" I wonder that, with your acquirements, you should have been content to remain in a state of slavery."

" Content ! " he repeated, bitterly. " Do you think I have been content? No, sir. Twice I attempted to escape. Each time I was caught, dragged back, and cruelly whipped. Then I was sold to the father of these little ones. He treated me so well, and I was getting so old, that I gave up the idea of running away."

" And where is he now."

" He became a colonel in the confederate service, and was killed at Antietam. Yesterday my mistress died, as I have told you."

" And are you left in sole charge of these little children ? "

" Yes, sir."

" Have they no relatives living ? "

" Their uncle lives in Kentucky. I shall try to carry them there."

" But you will find it hard work. You have only to cross the river, and in our lines you will be no longer a slave."

" I know it, sir. Three of my children have got their freedom, thank God, in that way. But I can't leave these children."

I looked down at them. They were beautiful little children. The youngest was a girl, with small features, dark hair, and black eyes. The boy, of six, was pale and composed, and uttered no murmur. Both clung confidently to the old negro.

I could not help admiring the old man, who could resist the prospect of freedom, though he had coveted it all his life, in order to remain loyal to his trust. I felt desirous of drawing him out on the subject of the war.

" What do you think of this war ? " I asked.

He lifted up his hand, and in a tone of solemnity, said, " I think it is the cloud by day, and the pillar of fire by night, that's going to draw us out of our bondage into the Promised Land."

I was struck by his answer.

" Do many of you — I mean of those who have not enjoyed your advantages of education — think so ? "

" Yes, sir ; we think it is the Lord's doings, and it is marvellous in our eyes. It's a time of trial and of tribulation; but it is n't a going to last. The children of Israel were forty years in the wilderness, and so it may be with us. The day of deliverance will come."

At this moment the little girl began again to cry, and he addressed himself to soothe her.

This was not the only group I encountered. Some women had come down to the river with children half bereft of their senses, — some apparently supposing that we should rob or murder them. The Rebel leaders and newspapers have so persistently reiterated these assertions, that they have come to believe them.

The third day was unusually lovely, but our hearts were too anxious to admit of our enjoying it. The Rebels were entrenched on heights behind the town. It was necessary that these should be taken, and about noon the movement commenced. Our forces marched steadily across the intervening plain. The Rebels reserved their fire till we were half-way across, and then from all sides burst forth the deadly fire. We were completely at their mercy. Twenty men in my own company fell dead or wounded, among them the captain and first lieutenant. Of what follows I can give you little idea. I gave myself up for lost. A desperate impulse enabled me to march on to what seemed certain destruction. All at once I felt a sensation of numbness in my left arm, and looking down I saw that the blood was trickling from it.

But I had little time to think of myself. Hearing a smothered groan, I looked round, and saw Frank Glover, pale and reeling.

"I'm shot in the leg," he said. "Don't leave me here. Help me along, and I will try to keep up with you."

The poor lad leaned upon me, and we staggered forward. But not for long. A stone wall stared us in the face. Here Rebel sharpshooters had been stationed, and they opened a galling fire upon us. We returned it, but what could we do? We were compelled to retire, and did so in good order, but unfortunately not until the sharpshooters had picked off some of our best men.

Among the victims was the poor lad whom I assisted. A second bullet struck him in the heart. He uttered just one word, "mother," and fell. Poor boy, and poor mother! He seemed to have a premonition of his approaching death, and requested me the day previous to take charge of his effects, and send them with his love and a lock of his hair to his mother if anything should befall him. This request I shall at once comply with. I have succeeded in getting the poor fellow's body brought to camp, where it will be decently buried, and have cut from his head two brown locks, one for his mother, and one for myself.

At last we got back with ranks fearfully diminished. Many old familiar faces were gone, — the faces of

16

those now lying stiff and stark in death. More were groaning with anguish in the crowded hospital. My own wound was too trifling to require much attention. I shall have to wear a sling for a few days perhaps.

There is little more to tell. Until Tuesday evening we maintained our position in daily expectation of an attack. But none was made. This was fortunate for us. I cannot understand what withheld the enemy from an assault.

On Tuesday suddenly came the order to recross the river. It was a stormy and dreary night, and so of course favorable to our purpose. The manœuvre was executed in silence, and with commendable expedition. The Rebels appeared to have no suspicion of General Burnside's intentions. The measured beat of our double quick was drowned by the fury of the storm, and with minds relieved, though bodies drenched, we once more found ourselves with the river between us and our foes. Nothing was left behind.

Here we are again, but not all of us. Many a brave soldier has breathed his last, and lies under the sod. "God's ways are dark, but soon or late they touch the shining hills of day." So sings our own Whittier, and so I believe, in spite of the sorrowful disaster which we have met with. It is all for the best if we could but see it.

Our heavy losses of officers have rendered some

new appointments necessary. Our second lieutenant has been made captain. The orderly sergeant and second sergeants are now our lieutenants, and the line of promotion has even reached me. I am a corporal.

I have been drawn into writing a very long letter, and I must now close, with the promise of writing again very soon. After I have concluded, I must write to poor Frank Glover's mother. May God comfort her, for she has lost a boy of whom any mother might feel proud.

With love to the children, I remain, as ever, your affectionate husband.

HENRY FROST.

"How terrible it must have been," said Mrs. Frost, with a shudder, as she folded up the letter and laid it down. "We ought indeed to feel thankful that your father's life was spared."

"If I were three years older, I might have been in the battle," thought Frank.

XXII.

FRANK BROACHES A NEW PLAN.

FOR some time Frank had been revolving in his mind the feasibility of a scheme which he hoped to be able to carry into execution. It was no less than this, — to form a military company among the boys, which should be organized and drilled in all respects like those composed of older persons. He did not feel like taking any steps in the matter till he had consulted with some one in whose judgment he had confidence.

One evening he mentioned his plan to Mr. Morton.

"It is a capital idea, Frank," said the young man, with warm approval. "If I can be of any service to you in this matter, it will afford me much pleasure."

"There is one difficulty," suggested Frank. "None of us boys knows anything about military tactics, and we shall need instruction to begin with; but where we are to find a teacher I am sure I can't tell."

"I don't think you will have to look far," said Mr. Morton, with a smile.

"Are you acquainted with the manual?" asked Frank, eagerly.

"I believe so. You see you have not yet got to the end of my accomplishments. I shall be happy to act as your drill-master until some one among your number is competent to take my place. I can previously give you some private lessons, if you desire it."

"There's nothing I should like better, Mr. Morton," said Frank, joyfully.

"Have you got a musket in the house, then? We shall get along better with one."

"There's one in the attic."

"Very well; if you will get it, we can make a beginning now."

Frank went in search of the musket; but in his haste tumbled down the attic stairs, losing his grasp of the musket, which fell down with a clatter.

Mrs. Frost, opening the door of her bedroom in alarm, saw Frank on his back with the musket lying across his chest.

"What's the matter?" she asked, not a little startled.

Frank got up rubbing himself and looking rather foolish.

"Nothing, mother; only I was in a little too much of a hurry."

"What are you going to do with that musket, Frank?"

16*

"Mr. Morton is going to teach me the manual, that is all, mother."

"I suppose the first position is horizontal," said his mother, with a smile.

"I don't like that position very well," returned Frank, with a laugh. "I prefer the perpendicular."

Under his friend's instructions, Frank progressed rapidly. At the end of the third lesson, Mr. Morton said, "You are nearly as competent to give instructions now as I am. There are some things, however, that cannot be learned alone. You had better take measures to form your company."

Frank called upon Mr. Rathburn, the Principal of the Academy, and after communicating his plan, which met with the teacher's full approval, arranged to have notice given of a meeting of the boys immediately after the afternoon session.

On Thursday afternoon when the last class had recited, previous to ringing the bell, which was a signal that school was over, Mr. Rathburn gave this brief notice.

"I am requested to ask the boys present to remain in their seats, to listen to a proposition that has my full approval, and in which I think they will all feel interested."

Looks of curiosity were interchanged among the boys, and every one thought, "What's coming now?"

At this moment a modest knock was heard, and

Mr. Rathburn, going to the door, admitted Frank. He quietly slipped into the nearest seat.

"Your late school-fellow, Frank Frost," proceeded Mr. Rathburn, "has the merit of orignating the plan to which I have referred, and he is no doubt prepared to unfold it to you."

Mr. Rathburn put on his hat and coat, and left the schoolroom. After his departure, Frank rose and spoke modestly, thus : —

"Boys, I have been thinking for some time past that we were not doing all that we ought in this crisis, which puts in such danger the welfare of our country. If anything, we boys ought to feel more deeply interested than our elders, for while they will soon pass off the stage we have not yet reached even the threshold of manhood. You will ask me what we can do. Let me remind you that when the war broke out, the great want was, not of volunteers, but of men trained to military exercises. Our regiments were at first composed wholly of raw recruits. In Europe, military instruction is given as a matter of course ; and in Germany, and perhaps other countries, young men are obliged to serve for a time in the army.

"I think we ought to profit by the lessons of experience. However the present war may turn out, we cannot be certain that other wars will not at some time break out. By that time we shall have grown to manhood, and the duty of defending our country

in arms will devolve upon us. Should that time
come, let it not find us unprepared. I propose that
we organize a military company among the boys,
and meet for drill at such times as we may hereafter
agree upon. I hope that any who feel interested in
the matter will express their opinions freely."

Frank sat down, and a number of the boys testi-
fied their approbation by stamping with their feet.

John Haynes rose with a sneer upon his face.

" I would humbly inquire, Mr. Chairman, for you
appear to have assumed that position, whether you
intend to favor us with your valuable services as
drill-master."

Frank rose with a flushed face.

" I am glad to be reminded of one thing, which I
had forgotten," he said.   " As this is a meeting for
the transaction of business, it is proper that it should
be regularly organized. Will some one nominate a
chairman ? "

" Frank Frost ! " exclaimed half a dozen voices.

" I thank you for the nomination," said Frank,
" but as I have something further to communicate to
the meeting, it will be better to select some one
else."

" I nominate Charles Reynolds," said one voice.

" Second the motion," said another.

" Those who are in favor of Charles Reynolds, as
Chairman of this meeting, will please signify it in the
usual manner," said Frank.

Charles Reynolds being declared duly elected, advanced to the teacher's chair.

"Mr. Chairman," said Frank, I will now answer the question, just put to me. I do not propose to offer my services as drill-master, but I am authorized to say that a gentleman whom you have all seen, Mr. Henry Morton, is willing to give instruction till you are sufficiently advanced to get along without it."

John Haynes, who felt disappointed at not having been called upon to preside over the meeting, determined to make as much trouble as possible.

"How are we to know that this Morton is qualified to give instruction?" he asked, looking round at the boys.

"The gentleman is out of order. He will please address his remarks to the Chair, and not to the audience," said the presiding officer.

"I beg pardon, Mr. Chairman," said John, mockingly. "I forgot how tenacious some people are of their brief authority."

"Order! order!" called half a dozen voices.

"The gentleman will come to order," said the Chairman, firmly; "and make way for others unless he can treat the Chair with proper respect."

"Mr. Chairman," said Frank, rising, "I will mention, for the general information, that Mr. Morton has acted as an officer of militia, and that I consider his offer a kind one, since it will take up considerable of his time and put him to some trouble."

"I move that Mr. Morton's offer be accepted with thanks," said Henry Tufts.

The motion was seconded by Tom Wheeler, and carried unanimously, with the exception of one vote. John Haynes sat sullenly in his seat and took no part in it.

"Who shall belong to the company?" asked the Chairman. "Shall a fixed age be required?"

"I move that the age be fixed at eleven," said Robert Ingalls.

This was objected to as too young, and twelve was finally fixed upon.

John Haynes moved not to admit any one who did not attend the Academy. Of course this would exclude Frank, and his motion was not seconded.

It was finally decided to admit any above the age of twelve who desired it; but the boys reserved to themselves the right of rejecting any who should conduct in a manner to bring disgrace upon them.

"Mr. Chairman," said Frank, "in order to get under way as soon as possible, I have written down an agreement to which those who wish to join our proposed company can sign their names. If anybody can think of anything better, I shall be glad to have it adopted instead of this."

He handed a sheet of paper to the Chairman, who read from it the following form of agreement: "We, the subscribers, agree to form a boys' volunteer company, and to conform to the regulations which may hereafter be made for its government."

"If there is no objection we will adopt this form, and subscribe our names," said the Chairman.

The motion for adoption being carried, the boys came up one by one, and signed their names.

John Haynes would have held back, but for the thought that he might be elected an officer of the new company.

"Is there any further business to come before the meeting?" inquired the presiding officer.

"What are we going to do for guns?" asked Robert Ingalls. "We can't get along without them."

"The boys at Webbington had a company three or four years ago," said Joe Barry, "and they used wooden guns."

"Wooden guns!" exclaimed Wilbur Summerfield, disdainfully. "You won't catch me training round town with a wooden gun."

"I would remind the last three gentlemen that their remarks should be addressed to the Chair," said the presiding officer. "Of course, I don't care anything about it, but I think you would all prefer to have the meeting conducted properly."

"That's so!" exclaimed several boys.

"Then," said the Chairman," I shall call to order any boy who addresses the meeting except through me."

" Mr. Chairman," said Frank, rising, " as to the wooden guns I quite agree with the last speaker. It would seem too much like boy's play, and we are too much in earnest for that. I have thought of an arrangement which can be made if the Selectmen will give their consent. Ten or fifteen years ago, longer than most of us can remember, as my father has told me, there was a militia company in Rossville, whose arms were supplied and owned by the town. When the company was disbanded the muskets went back to the town, and I believe they are now kept in the basement of the Town Hall. I presume that we can have the use of them on application. I move that a committee be appointed to lay the matter before the Selectmen, and ask their permission."

His motion was agreed to.

" I will appoint John Haynes to serve on that committee," said the Chairman, after a pause.

This was a politic appointment, as Squire Haynes was one of the Selectmen, and would be gratified at the compliment paid to his son.

" I accept the duty," said John, rising, and speaking in a tone of importance.

" Is there any other business to come before the meeting?"

" I should like to inquire, Mr. Chairman, when our first meeting will take place, and where is it to be?" asked Herbert Metcalf.

" I will appoint as a committee to make the necessary arrangements, Frank Frost, Tom Wheeler, and Robert Ingalls. Due notice will be given in school of the time and place selected, and a written notice will also be posted up in the Post-Office."

"Would it not be well, Mr. Chairman," suggested Frank, "to circulate an invitation to other boys not present to-day to join the company? The larger our numbers the more interest will be felt. I can think of quite a number who would be valuable members. — There are Dick Bumstead, and William Chamberlain, and many others."

At the sound of Dick Bumstead's name John Haynes looked askance at Frank; but for the moment the thought of Dick's agency in the affair of the pig-pen had escaped his recollection, and he looked quite unconscious of any indirect reference to it.

"Will you make a motion to that effect?"

"Yes, if necessary."

"Is the motion seconded?"

"Second it," said Moses Rogers.

"I will appoint Wilbur Summerfield and Moses Rogers on that committee," said the Chairman.

"I move that the meeting adjourn *ipse dixit*," said Sam Davis, bringing out the latter phrase with considerable emphasis.

A roar of laughter followed, which shook the schoolhouse to the very rafters, and then a deafening clamor of applause. The proposer sat down in confusion.

17

"What are you fellows laughing at?" he burst forth indignantly.

"Mr. Chairman," said Henry Tufts, struggling with his laughter, "I second the gentleman's motion, all except the Latin."

The motion was carried in spite of the manner in which it was worded, and the boys formed little groups, and began eagerly to discuss the plan which had been proposed. Frank had reason to feel satisfied with the success of his suggestion. Several of the boys came up to him, and expressed their pleasure that he had brought the matter before them.

"I say, Frank," said Robert Ingalls, "we'll have a bully company."

"Yes," said Wilbur Summerfield, "if John Haynes belongs to it. He's a bully, and no mistake."

"What's that you are saying about me?" blustered John Haynes, who caught a little of what was said.

"Listeners never hear anything good of themselves," answered Wilbur.

"Say that again, Wilbur Summerfield," said John, menacingly.

"Certainly, if it will do you any good. I said that you were a bully, John Haynes; and there's not a boy here that doesn't know it to be true."

"Take care!" said John, turning white with passion.

"While I'm about it, there's something more

I want to say," continued Wilbur, undauntedly. " Yesterday you knocked my little brother off his sled and sent him home crying. If you do it again you will have somebody else to deal with."

John trembled with anger. It would have done him good to " pitch into" Wilbur, but the latter looked him in the face so calmly and resolutely that discretion seemed to him the better part of valor, and with an oath he turned away.

" I don't know what's got into John Haynes," said Wilbur. " I never liked him, but now he seems to be getting worse and worse every day."

XXIII.

POMP TAKES MRS. PAYSON PRISONER.

OLD Mrs. Payson, who arrived in Rossville at the same time with Henry Morton, had been invited by her daughter, "Cynthy Ann," to pass the winter, and had acquiesced without making any very strenuous objections. Her "bunnit," which she had looked upon as "sp'ilt," had been so far restored by a skilful milliner that she was able to wear it for best. As this restoration cost but one dollar and a half out of the five which had been given her by young Morton, she felt very well satisfied with the way matters had turned out. This did not, however, by any means diminish her rancor against Pomp, who had been the mischievous cause of the calamity.

"Ef I could only get hold on him," Mrs. Payson had remarked on several occasions to Cynthy Ann, "I'd shake the mischief out of him ef I died for 't the very next minute."

Mrs. Payson was destined to meet with a second calamity, which increased, if possible, her antipathy to the "young imp."

Being of a social disposition, she was quite in the

habit of dropping in to tea at different houses in the village. Having formerly lived in Rossville, she was acquainted with nearly all the towns people, and went the rounds about once in two weeks.

One afternoon she put her knitting into a black workbag, which she was accustomed to carry on her arm, and arraying herself in a green cloak and hood, which had served her for fifteen years, she set out to call on Mrs. Thompson.

Now, the nearest route to the place of her destination lay across a five-acre lot. The snow lay deep upon the ground, but the outer surface had become so hard as, without difficulty, to bear a person of ordinary weight.

When Mrs. Payson came up to the bars, she said to herself, " 'T ain't so fur to go across lots. I guess I 'll ventur'."

She let down a bar, and passing through, went on her way complacently. But, alas, for the old lady's peace of mind! She was destined to come to very deep grief.

That very afternoon Pomp had come over to play with Sam Thompson, and the two, after devising various projects of amusement, had determined to make a cave in the snow. They selected a part of the field where it had drifted to the depth of some four or five feet. Beginning at a little distance, they burrowed their way into the heart of the snow, and excavated a place about four feet square by four deep,

17*

leaving the upper crust intact, of course without its ordinary strength.

The two boys had completed their task, and were sitting down in their subterranean abode, when the roof suddenly gave way and a visitor entered in the most unceremonious manner.

The old lady had kept on her way unsuspiciously, using as a cane a faded blue umbrella, which she carried invariably, whatever the weather.

When Mrs. Payson felt herself sinking, she uttered a loud shriek and waved her arms aloft, brandishing her umbrella in a frantic way. She was plunged up to her arm-pits in the snow, and was of course placed in a very unfavorable position for extricating herself.

The two boys were at first nearly smothered by the descent of snow, but when the first surprise was over they recognized their prisoner. I am ashamed to say that their first feeling was that of unbounded delight, and they burst into a roar of laughter. The sound, indistinctly heard, terrified the old lady beyond measure, and she struggled frantically to escape, nearly poking out Pomp's eye with the point of her umbrella.

Pomp, always prompt to repel aggression, in return, pinched her foot.

"Massy sakes! Where am I?" ejaculated the affrighted old lady. "There's some wild crittur down there. O, Cynthy Ann, ef you could see your marm at this moment!"

She made another vigorous flounder and managed to kick Sam in the face. Partly as a measure of self-defence he seized her ancle firmly.

"He's got hold of me!" shrieked the old lady. "Help! help! I shall be murdered."

Her struggles became so energetic that the boys soon found it expedient to evacuate the premises. They crawled out by the passage they had made, and appeared on the surface of the snow.

The old lady presented a ludicrous appearance. Her hood had slipped off, her spectacles were resting on the end of her nose, and she had lost her work-bag. But she clung with the most desperate energy to the umbrella, on which apparently depended her sole hope of deliverance.

"Hi yah!" laughed Pomp, as he threw himself back on the snow, and began to roll about in an ecstasy of delight.

Instantly Mrs. Payson's apprehensions changed to furious anger.

"So it's you, you little varmint, that's done this. Jest le' me get out, and I'll whip you so you can't stan'. See ef I don't."

"You can't get out, missus; yah, yah!" laughed Pomp. "You's tied, you is, missus."

"Come an' help me out, this minute!" exclaimed the old lady, stamping her foot.

"Lor', missus, you'll whip me. You said you would."

" So I will, I vum," retorted the irate old lady, rather undiplomatically. " As true as I live, I'll whip you till you can't stan'."

As she spoke, she brandished her umbrella in a menacing manner.

" Den, missus, I guess you'd better stay where you is."

" O, you imp! See ef I don't have you put in jail. Here, you, Sam Thompson, come and help me out. Ef you don't, I'll tell your mother, an' she'll give you the wust lickin' you ever had. I'm surprised at you."

" You won't tell of me, will you?" said Sam, irresolutely.

" I'll see about it," said the old lady, in a politic tone.

She felt her powerlessness, and that concession must precede victory.

" Then, give me the umbrella," said Sam, who evidently distrusted her.

" You'll run off with it," said Mrs. Payson, suspiciously.

" No; I won't."

" Well, there 'tis."

" Come here, Pomp, and help me," said Sam.
Pomp held aloof.

" She'll whip me," he said, shaking his head. " She's an old debble."

" O you — you sarpint!" ejaculated the old lady, almost speechless with indignation.

"You can run away as soon as she gets out," suggested Sam.

Pomp advanced slowly and warily, rolling his eyes in indecision.

"Jest catch hold of my hands, both on ye," said Mrs. Payson, "an' I'll give a jump."

These directions were followed, and the old lady rose to the surface, when, in an evil hour, intent upon avenging herself upon Pomp, she made a clutch for his collar. In doing so, she lost her footing and fell back into the pit from which she had just emerged. Her spectacles dropped off, and falling beneath her were broken.

She rose, half provoked and half ashamed of her futile attempt. It was natural that neither of these circumstances should effect an improvement in her temper.

"You did it a purpose," she said, shaking her fist at Pomp, who stood about a rod off grinning at her discomfiture. "There, I've gone an' broke my specs, that I bought two years ago, come fall, of a pedler. I'll make you pay for 'em."

"Lor', missus, I ain't got no money," said Pomp. "Nebber had none."

Unfortunately for the old lady, it was altogether probable that Pomp spoke the truth this time.

"Three an' sixpence gone!" groaned Mrs. Payson. "Fust my bunnit, an' then my specs. I'm the most unfort'nit' critter. Why don't you help me out, Sam Thompson, instead of standin' and gawkin' at me?" she suddenly exclaimed, glaring at Sam.

"I did n't know as you was ready," said Sam. "You might have been out before this, ef you had n't let go. Here, Pomp, lend a hand."

Pomp shook his head decisively.

"Don't catch dis chile again," he said. "I'm goin' home. Old woman wants to lick me."

Sam endeavored to persuade Pomp, but he was deaf to persuasion. He squatted down on the snow, and watched the efforts his companion made to extricate the old lady. When she was nearly out he started on a run, and was at a safe distance before Mrs. Payson was in a situation to pursue him.

The old lady shook herself to make sure that no bones were broken. Next, she sent Sam down into the hole to pick up her bag, and then finding, on a careful examination, that she had recovered everything, even to the blue umbrella, fetched the astonished Sam a rousing box on the ear.

"What did you do that for?" he demanded in an aggrieved tone.

"'Tain't half as much as you deserve," said the old lady. "I'm goin' to your house right off, to tell your mother what you 've been a doin'. Ef you was my child, I 'd beat you black and blue."

"I wish I 'd left you down there," muttered Sam.

" What's that?" demanded Mrs. Payson, sharply.
" Don't you go to bein' sassy. It'll be the wuss for
ye. You'll come to the gallows some time, ef you
don't mind your P's and Q's. I might 'ave stayed
there till I died, an' then you'd have been hung."

" What are you jawing about?" retorted Sam.
" How could I know you was comin'?"

" You know'd it well enough," returned the old
lady. " You'll bring your mother's gray hairs with
sorrer to the grave."

" She ain't got any gray hairs," said Sam, dog-
gedly.

" Well, she will have some, ef she lives long
enough. I once know'd a boy jest like you, an' he
was put in jail for stealin'."

" I ain't a goin' to stay and be jawed that way,"
said Sam. " You won't catch me pulling you out of
a hole again. I wouldn't have you for a grandmother for all the world. Tom Baldwin told me,
only yesterday, that you was always a hectorin' him."

Tom Baldwin was the son of Cynthy Ann, and
consequently old Mrs. Payson's grandson.

" Did Tom Baldwin tell you that?" demanded the
old lady abruptly, looking deeply incensed.

" Yes, he did."

" Well, he's the ungratefullest cub that I ever
sot eyes on," exclaimed his indignant grandmother.
" Arter all I've done for him. I'm knittin' a pair
of socks for him this blessed minute. But he shan't

have 'em.   I'll give 'em to the soldiers, I vum.
Did he say anything else?"

"Yes, he said he should be glad when you were
gone."

"I'll go right home and tell Cynthy Ann," exclaimed Mrs. Payson, "an' ef she don't w'ip him I
will.   I never see such a bad set of boys as is
growin' up.   There ain't one on 'em that is n't as full
of mischief as a nut is of meat.   I'll come up with
them, as true as I live."

Full of her new indignation, Mrs. Payson gave up
her proposed call on Mrs. Thompson, and turning
about, hurried home to lay her complaint before
Cynthy Ann.

"I'm glad she's gone," said Sam, looking after
her, as with resolute steps she trudged along, punch-
ing the snow vigorously with the point of her blue
cotton umbrella.   "I pity Tom Baldwin; if I had
such a grandmother as that I'd run away to sea.
That's so!"

XXIV.

A CHAPTER FROM HARDEE.

A FEW rods east of the post-office, on the opposite side of the street, was a two-story building used as an Engine House. The second story consisted of a hall used for company meetings. This the fire company obligingly granted to the boys as a drill-room during the inclement season, until the weather became sufficiently warm to drill out of doors.

On the Monday afternoon succeeding the preliminary meeting at the Academy, about thirty boys assembled in this hall, pursuant to a notice which had been given at school and posted up at the tavern and post-office.

At half-past two Frank entered accompanied by Mr. Morton.

Some of the boys were already acquainted with him, and came up to speak. He had a frank cordial way with boys which secured their favor at first sight.

"Well, boys," said he, pleasantly, "I believe I am expected to make soldiers of you."

"Yes, sir," said Charles Reynolds, respectfully,

18

"I hope we shall learn readily, and do credit to your instructions."

"I have no fear on that score," was the reply. "Perhaps you may have some business to transact before we commence our lessons. If so I will sit down a few moments, and wait till you are ready."

A short business meeting was held, organized as before.

John Haynes reported that he had spoken to his father, and the question of allowing the boys the use of the muskets belonging to the town would be acted upon at the next meeting of the selectmen. Squire Haynes thought that the request would be granted.

"What are we going to do this afternoon?" asked Robert Ingalls.

"I can answer that question, Mr. Chairman," said Henry Morton. "We are not yet ready for muskets. I shall have to drill you first in the proper position of a soldier, and the military step. Probably it will be a week before I shall wish to place muskets into your hands. May I inquire how soon there will be a meeting of the selectmen?"

John Haynes announced that the next meeting would be holden in less than a week.

"Then there will be no difficulty as to the muskets," said Mr. Morton.

Wilbur Summerfield reported that he had extended an invitation to boys not connected with the Academy

to join the Company. Several were now present.
Dick Bumstead, though not able to attend that day,
would come to the next meeting. He thought they
would be able to raise a company of fifty boys.

This report was considered very satisfactory.

Tom Wheeler arose and inquired by what name
the new company would be called.

"I move," said Robert Ingalls, "that we take
the name of the Rossville Home Guards."

"If the enemy should invade Rossville, you'd be
the first to run," sneered John Haynes.

"Not unless I heard of it before you," was the
quick reply.

There was a general laugh, and cries of "Bully
for you, Bob," were heard.

"Order!" cried the Chairman, pounding the table
energetically. "Such disputes cannot be allowed.
I think we had better defer obtaining a name for our
company till we find how well we are likely to succeed."

This proposal seemed to be acquiesced in by the
boys generally. The business meeting terminated,
and Mr. Morton was invited to commence his instructions.

"The boys will please form themselves in a line,"
said the teacher, in a clear commanding voice.

This was done.

The positions assumed were, most of them, far
from military. Some stood with their legs too far

apart, others with one behind the other, some with the shoulders of unequal height. Frank alone stood correctly, thanks to the private instructions he had received.

"Now, boys," said Mr. Morton, "when I say 'Attention,' you must all look at me and follow my directions implicitly. Attention and subordination are of the first importance to a soldier. Let me say, to begin with, that, with one exception, you are all standing wrong."

Here there was a general shifting of positions. Robert Ingalls who had been standing with his feet fifteen inches apart, suddenly brought them close together in a parallel position. Tom Wheeler, who had been resting his weight mainly on the left foot shifted to the right. Moses Rogers whose head was bent over so as to watch his feet, now threw it so far back that he seemed to be inspecting the ceiling. Frank alone remained stationary.

Mr. Morton smiled at the changes elicited by his remarks, and proceeded to give his first command.

"Heels on the same line!" he ordered.

All the boys turned their heads, and there was a noisy shuffling of feet.

"Quit crowding, Tom Baldwin!" exclaimed Sam Rivers in an audible tone.

"Quit crowding yourself," was the reply. "You've got more room than I now."

"Silence in the ranks!" said the instructor authoritatively. "Frank Frost, I desire you to see that the boys stand at regular distances."

This was accomplished.

"Turn out your feet equally so as to form a right angle with each other. So."

Mr. Morton illustrated his meaning practically. This was very necessary as some of the boys had very confused ideas as to what was meant by a right angle.

After some time this order was satisfactorily carried out.

"The knees must be straight. I see that some are bent as if the weight of the body were too much for them. Not too stiff! Rivers, yours are too rigid. You could n't walk a mile in that way without becoming very tired. There, that is much better. Notice my position."

The boys after adjusting their positions looked at the rest to see how they had succeeded.

"Don't look at each other," said Mr. Morton. "If you do you will be certain to make blunders. I notice that some of you are standing with one shoulder higher than the other. The shoulders should be square, and the body should be erect upon the hips. Attention! So!"

"Very well. Haynes, you are trying to stand too upright. You must not bend backwards. All, incline your bodies a little forward. Frank Ingalls is standing correctly."

18*

"I don't think that's very soldierly," said John Haynes, who felt mortified at being corrected, having flattered himself that he was right and the rest were wrong.

"A soldier should n't be round-shouldered, or have a slouching gait," said the instructor, quietly; "but you will find when you come to march that the opposite extreme is attended with great inconvenience and discomfort. Until then you must depend upon my assurance."

Mr. Morton ran his eyes along the line, and observed that most of the boys were troubled about their arms. Some allowed them to hang in stiff rigidity by their sides. One, even, had his clasped behind his back. Others let theirs dangle loosely, swinging now hither, now thither.

He commented upon these errors, and added, "let your arms hang naturally, with the elbows near the body, the palm of the hand a little turned to the front, the little finger behind the seam of the pantaloons. This you will find important when you come to drill with muskets. You will find that it will economize space by preventing your occupying more room than is necessary. Frank, will you show Sam Rivers and John Haynes how to hold their hands?"

"You need n't trouble yourself," said John, haughtily, but in too low a voice, as he supposed, for Mr. Morton to hear. "I don't want a clodhopper to teach me."

Frank's face flushed slightly, and without a word he passed John, and occupied himself with showing Sam Rivers, who proved more tractable.

" No talking in the ranks ! " said Mr. Morton, in a tone of authority. " If any boy wishes to ask any explanation of me he may do so, but it is a breach of discipline to speak to each other."

" My next order will be, — faces to the front ! " he resumed after a pause. " Nothing looks worse than to see a file of men with their heads turned in various directions. The eyes should be fixed straight before you, striking the ground at about fifteen paces forward."

It required some time to have this direction properly carried out. Half an hour had now passed, and some of the boys showed signs of weariness.

" I will now give you a little breathing-spell for ten minutes," said Mr. Morton. " After this we will resume our exercises."

The boys stretched their limbs, and began to converse in an animated strain about the lesson which they had just received.

At the expiration of ten minutes the lesson was resumed, and some additional directions were given.

It will not be necessary for us to follow the boys during the remainder of the lesson. Most of them made very creditable progress, and the line presented quite a different appearance at the end of the exercise from what it had at the commencement.

"I shall be prepared to give you a second lesson on Saturday afternoon," announced Mr. Morton. "In the mean time it will be well for you to remember what I have said, and if you should feel inclined to practise by yourselves, it will no doubt make your progress more rapid."

These remarks were followed by a clapping of hands on the part of the boys, — a demonstration of applause which Mr. Morton acknowledged by a bow and a smile.

"Well, how do you like it?" asked Frank Frost of Robert Ingalls.

"O, it's bully fun!" returned Bob, enthusiastically. "I feel like a hero already."

"You're as much of one now, Bob, as you'll ever be," said Wilbur, good naturedly.

"I wouldn't advise you to be a soldier," retorted Bob. "You're too fat to run, and would be too frightened to fight."

"I certainly couldn't expect to keep up with those long legs of yours, Bob," said Wilbur, laughing.

The boys dispersed in excellent humor, fully determined to persevere in their military exercises.

XXV.

ELECTION OF OFFICERS.

FOR the six weeks following Mr. Morton gave lessons twice a week to the boys. At the third lesson they received their muskets, and thenceforth drilled with them. A few who had not been present at the first two lessons, and were consequently ignorant of the positions, Mr. Morton turned over to Frank, who proved an efficient and competent instructor.

At the end of the twelfth lesson, Mr. Morton, after giving the order " Rest ! " addressed the boys as follows : —

" Boys, we have now taken twelve lessons together. I have been very much gratified by the rapid improvement which you have made, and feel that it is due quite as much to your attention as to any instructions of mine. I can say with truth that I have known companies of grown men who have made less rapid progress than you.

" The time has now come when I feel that I can safely leave you to yourselves. There are those among you who are competent to carry on the work

which I have commenced. It will be desirable for
you at once to form a company organization. As
there are but fifty on your muster-roll, being about
half the usual number, you will not require as many
officers. I recommend the election of a Captain, first
and second lieutenants, three sergeants and three cor-
porals. You have already become somewhat accustomed to company drill, so that you will be able to go
on by yourselves under the guidance of your officers.
If any doubtful questions should arise, I shall always
be happy to give you any information or assistance in
my power.

"And now, boys, I will bid you farewell in my
capacity of instructor; but I need not say that I
shall continue to watch with interest your progress in
the military art."

Here Mr. Morton bowed, and sat down.

After the applause which followed his speech had
subsided, there was a silence and hush of expectation
among the boys, after which Charles Reynolds rose
slowly, and taking from the seat beside him a pack-
age, advanced towards Mr. Morton, and made a brief
speech of presentation, having been deputed by the
boys to perform that duty.

" MR. MORTON : —

" I stand here in behalf of the boys present, who
wish to express to you their sense of your kindness

in giving them the course of lessons which has just ended. We have taken up much of your time, and no doubt have tried your patience more than once. If we have improved, as you were kind enough to . say, we feel that it is principally owing to our good fortune in having so skilful a teacher. We wish to present you some testimonial of the regard which we have for you, and accordingly ask your acceptance of this copy of ' Abbott's Life of Napoleon.' We should have been glad to give you something more valuable, but we are sure you will value the gift for other reasons than its cost."

Here Charles Reynolds sat down, and all eyes were turned towards Mr. Morton. It was evident that he was taken by surprise. It was equally evident that he was much gratified by this unexpected token of regard.

He rose and with much feeling spoke as follows:

" My dear boys, for you must allow me to call you so, I can hardly tell you how much pleasure your kind gift has afforded me. It gives me the assurance, which indeed I did not need, that you are as much my friends as I am yours. The connection between us has afforded me much pleasure and satisfaction. In training you to duties which patriotism may here-after devolve upon you, (though I pray Heaven that long before that time our terrible civil strife may be at an end,) I feel that I have helped you to do something to show your loyal devotion to the country which we all love and revere. (Here there was loud applause.) If you were a few years older I doubt not that your efforts would be added to those of your fathers and brothers who are now encountering the perils and suffering the privations of war. And with a little practice I am proud to say that you would not need to be ashamed of the figure you would cut in the field.

"I have little more to say. I recognize a fitness in the selection of the work which you have given me. Napoleon is without doubt the greatest military genius which our modern age has produced. Yet he lacked one very essential characteristic of a good soldier. He was more devoted to his own selfish ends than to the welfare of his country. I shall value your gift for the good wishes that accompany it, and the recollection of this day will be among my pleasantest memories."

Mr. Morton here withdrew in the midst of hearty applause.

When he had left the hall a temporary organization for business purposes was at once effected. Wilbur Summerfield was placed in the Chair, and the meeting proceeded at once to an election of officers.

For a week or two past there had been consider-

able private canvassing among the boys. There
were several who would like to have been elected
Captain, and a number of others, who, though not
aspiring so high, hoped to be first or second lieutenants. Among the first class was John Haynes.
Like many persons who are unpopular, he did not
seem to be at all aware of the extent of his unpopularity.

But there was another weighty reason why the
choice of the boys would never have fallen upon
him. Apart from his unpopularity, he was incompetent for the posts to which he aspired. Probably
there were not ten boys in the company who were
not more proficient in drill than he. This was not
owing to any want of natural capacity, but to a
feeling that he did not require much instruction, and
a consequent lack of attention to the directions of
Mr. Morton. He had frequently been corrected in
mistakes, but always received the correction with
sullenness and impatience. He felt in his own mind
that he was much better fitted to govern than to
obey; forgetting in his ambition that it is those only
who have first learned to obey who are best qualified
to rule others.

Desirous of ingratiating himself with the boys,
and so securing their votes, he had been unusually
amiable and generous during the past week. At the
previous lesson, he had brought half a bushel of
apples from which he had requested the boys to help

19

themselves freely.   By this means he hoped to attain the object of his ambition.

Squire Haynes, too, was interested in the success of his son.

" If they elect you Captain, John," he promised, " I will furnish you money enough to buy a handsome sash and sword."

Besides John, there were several others who cherished secret hopes of success.   Among these were Charles Reynolds and Wilbur Summerfield. As for Frank Frost, though he had thought little about it, he could not help feeling that he was among those best qualified for office, though he would have been quite content with either of the three highest offices, or even with the post of orderly sergeant.

Among those who had acquitted themselves with the greatest credit was our old friend Dick Bumstead, whom we remember last as concerned in rather a questionable adventure.   Since that time his general behavior had very much changed for the better. Before, he had always shirked work when it was possible.   Now he exhibited a steadiness and industry which surprised no less than it gratified his father.

This change was partly owing to his having given up some companions who had done him no good, and instead, sought the society of Frank.   The energy and manliness exhibited by his new friend, and the sensible views which he took of life and duty, had wrought quite a revolution in Dick's character.   He began to see that if he ever meant to accomplish anything he must begin now. At Frank's instance he had giving up smoking, and this cut off one of the temptations which had assailed him. Gradually the opinion entertained of Dick in the village as a ne'er-do-well was modified, and he had come to be classed as one of the steady and reliable boys — a reputation not to be lightly regarded.

In the present election Dick did not dream that he could have any interest. While he had been interested in the lessons, and done his best, he felt that his previous reputation would injure his chances, and he had made up his mind that he should have to serve in the ranks. This did not trouble him, for Dick, to his credit be it said, was very free from jealousy, and had not a particle of envy in his composition. He possessed so many good qualities that it would have been a thousand pities if he had kept on in his former course.

"You will bring in your votes for Captain," said the Chairman.

Tom Wheeler distributed slips of paper among the boys, and there was forthwith a plentiful show of pencils.

"Are the votes all in?" inquired the Chairman, a little late. "If so, we will proceed to count them."

There was a general hush of expectation while Wilbur Summerfield, the Chairman, and Robert Ingalls, the Secretary of the meeting, were counting the votes. John Haynes was evidently nervous, and fidgeted about anxious to learn his fate.

At length the count was completed, and Wilbur rising announced it as follows : —

Whole number of votes . . 49.
Necessary for a choice . . 25.
Robert Ingalls . . . 2 votes.
John Haynes . . . . 2 "
Wilbur Summerfield . . 4 "
Moses Rogers . . . . 4 "
Charles Reynolds . . . 10 "
Frank Frost . . . . 27 "

" Gentlemen, I have the pleasure of announcing that you have made choice of Frank Frost as your Captain."

Frank rose amid a general clapping of hands, and with heightened color but modest self-possession, spoke as follows : " Boys, I thank you very much for this proof of your confidence. All I can say is that I will endeavor to deserve it. I shall no doubt make some mistakes, but I feel sure that you will grant me your indulgence, and not expect too much of my inexperience."

This speech was regarded with favor by all except John Haynes, who would rather have had any one else elected, independent of his own disappointment, which was great.

" You will now prepare your votes for First Lieutenant," said the presiding officer.

It will be noticed that two votes were cast for John Haynes. One of these was thrown by a competitor who wished to give his vote to some one who stood no possible chance of succeeding, and accordingly selected John on account of his well-known unpopularity. This vote therefore was far from being a compliment. As for the other vote John Haynes himself best knew by whom it was cast.

The boys began to prepare their votes for first lieutenant.

John brightened up a little. He felt that it would be something to gain this office. But when the result of the balloting was announced, it proved that he had but a single vote.

There were several scattering votes. The two prominent candidates were Dick Bumstead who received eight votes, and Charles Reynolds who received thirty-two, and was accordingly declared elected.

No one was more surprised by this announcement than Dick. He felt quite bewildered, not having the slightest expectation of being a candidate. He was almost tempted to believe that the votes had only been cast in jest.

But Dick was destined to a still greater surprise. At the next vote for second lieutenant there were five scattering votes. Then came ten for Wilbur Summerfield, and Richard Bumstead led off

19*

with thirty-four, and was accordingly declared duly elected.

" Speech ! Speech ! " exclaimed half a dozen, vociferously.

Dick looked a little confused, and tried to escape the call. But the boys were determined to have him up, and he was finally compelled to rise, looking and feeling rather awkward. But his natural good sense and straightforwardness came to his aid, and he acquitted himself quite creditably.

This was Dick's speech.

" Boys, I don't know how to make speeches, and I s'pose you know that as well as I do. I hardly knew who was meant when Richard Bumstead's name was mentioned, having always been called Dick ; but if it means me, all I can say is, that I am very much obliged to you for the unexpected honor. One reason why I did not expect to be elected to any office was because I ain't as good a scholar as most of you. I am sure there are a great many of you who would make better officers than I, but I don't think there 's any that will try harder to do well than I shall."

Here Dick sat down, very much astonished to find that he had actually made a speech. His speech was modest, and made a favorable impression, as was shown by the noisy stamping of feet, and shouts of " Bully for you, Dick ! " " You 're a trump ! " and other terms in which boys are wont to signify their approbation.

Through all this John Haynes looked very much disgusted, and seemed half decided upon leaving the room. He had some curiosity, however, to learn who would be elected to the subordinate offices, and so remained. He had come into the room with the determination not **to** accept anything below a lieutenancy, but now made up his mind not to reject the post of orderly sergeant if it should be offered to him. The following list of officers, however, will show that he was allowed no choice in the matter.

Captain, Frank Frost.
First Lieutenant, Charles Reynolds.
Second Lieutenant, Richard Bumstead.
Orderly Sergeant, Wilbur Summerfield.
Second Sergeant, Robert Ingalls.
Third Sergeant, Moses Rogers.
First Corporal, Tom Wheeler.
Second Corporal, Joseph Barry.
Third Corporal, Frank Ingalls.

The entire list of officers was now read, and received with applause. If there were some who were disappointed, they acquiesced good-naturedly, with one exception.

When the applause had subsided, John Haynes rose, and in a voice trembling with passion, said : —

" Mr. Chairman, I wish to give notice to all present that I resign my place as a member of this Com-

pany.   I don't choose·to serve under such officers as
you have chosen to-day.   I don't think they are fit
to have command."

Here there was a general chorus of hisses, drowning John's voice completely.   After glancing about
him a moment in speechless fury, he seized his hat,
and left the room in indignant haste, slamming the
door after him.

"He's a mean fellow!" said Frank Ingalls.   "I
suppose he expected to be Captain."

"Should n't wonder," said Sam Rivers.   "Any-
how, he's a fool to make such a fuss about it.   As
for me," he added, with a mirthful glance, "I am
just as much disappointed as he is.   When I came
here this afternoon I expected I should be elected
Captain, and I'd got my speech all ready ; but now
I'm sorry that it will have to be wasted."

There was a general burst of laughter, for Sam
Rivers, whom everybody liked for his good nature,
was incorrigibly awkward, and had made a larger
number of blunders, probably, than any other member of the Company.

"Give us the speech, Sam," said Bob Ingalls.

"Yes, don't let it be wasted."

"Speech, speech!" cried Joseph Barry.

"Very well, gentlemen, if you desire it."

Sam drew from his pocket a blank piece of paper,
and pretended to read the following speech, which he
made up on the spur of the moment.

" Ahem ! gentlemen," he commenced, in a pompous tone, assuming an air of importance : " I am deeply indebted to you for this very unexpected honor."

" O, *very*," said one of the boys near.

" I feel that you have done yourself credit in your selection."

Here there was a round of applause.

" I am sorry that some of you are still very **awkward**, but I hope under my excellent discipline **to** make veterans of you in less than no time."

" Good for you ! "

" You cannot expect me to remain long with you, as I am now in the line of promotion, and don't mean to stop short of a brigadier. But as long as I am your Captain, I hope you will appreciate your privileges."

Sam's speech was followed by a chorus of laughter, in which he joined heartily himself.

As for John's defection nobody seemed to regret it much. It was generally felt that the Company would have no difficulty in getting along without him.

XXVI.

THE REBEL TRAP.

ON the first of April Frank received the following letter from his father. It was the more welcome because nearly a month had elaped since anything had been received, and the whole family had become quite anxious.

DEAR FRANK (the letter commenced), you are no doubt feeling anxious on account of my long silence. You will understand the cause of it when I tell you that since the date of my last letter I have been for a fortnight in the enemy's hands as a prisoner. Fortunately I have succeeded in effecting my escape. You will naturally be interested to learn the particulars.

Three weeks since, a lady occupying an estate 'about five miles distant from our camp, waited on our commanding officer and made an urgent request to have a few soldiers detailed as a guard to protect her and her property from molestation and loss. Our colonel was not at first disposed to grant her request, but finally acceded to it, rather reluctantly, declaring that it was all nonsense. I was selected,

with five other men, to serve as a guard. Mrs.
Roberts — for this was her name — appeared quite
gratified to find her request granted, and drove
slowly home under our escort.

On arriving, we found a mansion in the old
Virginia style, low in elevation, broad upon the
ground, and with a piazza extending along the
front. Surrounding it was a good-sized plantation. At a little distance from the house was a
row of negro huts. These were mostly vacant, —
the former occupants having secured their freedom
by taking refuge within our lines.

As sergeant in command (you must know that
I have been promoted), I inquired of Mrs. Roberts
what danger she apprehended. Her answers were
vague and unsatisfactory. However, she seemed
disposed to treat me very civilly, and at nine o'clock
invited the whole party into the house to partake of
a little refreshment. This invitation was very welcome to soldiers who had not for months partaken of
anything better than camp fare. It was all the more
acceptable because outside a cold rain was falling,
and the mud was deep and miry.

In the dining-room we found a plentiful meal
spread, including hot coffee, hot corn-bread, bacon,
and other viands. We were not, however, destined
to take our supper in peace. As I was drinking my
second cup of coffee I thought I heard a noise outside, and remarked it to Mrs. Roberts.

"It is only the wind, sergeant," said she, indifferently.

It was not long before I became convinced that it was something more serious. I ordered my men to stand to their arms, in spite of the urgent protestations of the old lady, and marched them out upon the lawn, just in time to be confronted by twenty or thirty men on horseback, clad in the Rebel uniform.

Resistance against such odds would have been only productive of useless loss of life, and with my little force I was compelled to surrender myself a prisoner.

Of course I no longer doubted that we were the victims of a trick, and had been lured by Mrs. Roberts purposely to be made prisoners. If I had had any doubts on the subject, her conduct would have dissipated them. She received our captors with open arms. They stepped into our places as guests, and the house was thrown open to them. Our arms were taken from us, our hands were pinioned, and a scene of festivity ensued. A cask of wine was brought up from the cellar, and the contents freely distributed among the Rebels, or grey backs, as we call them here.

Once, as Mrs. Roberts passed through the little room where we were confined, I said, "Do you consider this honorable conduct, madam, to lure us here by false representations, and then betray us to our enemies?"

"Yes, I do!" said she, hotly. "What business have you to come down here and lay waste our territory? There is no true Southern woman but despises you heartily, and would do as much as I have, and more, too. You've got my son a prisoner in one of your Yankee prisons. When I heard that he was taken, I swore to be revenged; and I have kept my word. I've got ten for one, though he's worth a hundred such as you!"

So saying, she swept out of the room, with a scornful look of triumph in her eyes. The next day, as I afterwards learned, she sent word to our colonel that her house had been unexpectedly attacked by a large party of the Rebels, and that we had been taken prisoners. Her complicity was suspected, but was not proved till our return to the camp. Of course, a further guard, which she asked for, to divert suspicion, was refused.

Meanwhile we were carried some twenty miles across the river, and confined in a building which had formerly been used as a storehouse.

The place was dark and gloomy. There were some dozen others who shared our captivity. Here we had rather a doleful time. We were supplied with food three times a day; but the supply was scanty, and we had meat but once in two days. We gathered that it was intended to send us to Richmond; but from day to day there was a delay in doing so. We decided that our chance of escape would

20

be much better then than after we reached the Rebel
capital. We therefore formed a plan for defeating
the intentions of our captors.

Though the building assigned to us as a prison
consisted of two stories, we were confined in the
lower part. This was more favorable to our designs.
During the night we busied ourselves in loosening
two of the planks of the flooring, so that we could
remove them at any time. Then lowering two of
our number into the cellar, we succeeded in remov-
ing enough of the stone foundation to allow the escape of one man at a time through the aperture.
Our arrangements were hastened by the assignment
of a particular day on which we were to be trans-
ferred from our prison, and conveyed to Richmond.
Though we should have been glad to enter the city
under some circumstances, we did not feel very desirous of going as prisoners of war.

On the night selected we waited impatiently till
midnight. Then, as silently as possible, we removed
the planking, and afterwards the stones of the basement wall, and crept through one by one. All this
was effected so noiselessly that we were all out without creating any alarm. We could hear the measured tramp of the sentinel, as he paced up and down
in front of the empty prison. We pictured to ourselves his surprise when he discovered, the next
morning, that we had escaped under his nose without his knowing it !

I need not dwell upon the next twenty-four hours. The utmost vigilance was required to elude the Rebel pickets. At last, after nearly twenty hours, during which we had had nothing to eat, we walked into camp, exhausted with hunger and fatigue, to the great joy of our comrades from whom we had been absent a fortnight.

On receiving information of the manner in which we had been captured, our commanding officer at once despatched me with a detachment of men to arrest Mrs. Roberts and her daughter. Her surprise and dismay at seeing me whom she supposed safe in Richmond were intense. She is still under arrest.

I suppose our campaign will open as soon as the roads are dried up. The mud in Virginia is much more formidable than at the North, and presents an insuperable, perhaps I should say an unfathomable obstacle to active operations. I hope General Grant will succeed in taking Vicksburg. The loss of that important stronghold would be a great blow to the Rebels.

You ask me, in your last letter, whether I see much of the contrabands. I have talked with a considerable number. One, a very intelligent fellow, had been very much trusted by his master, and had accompanied him to various parts of the South. I asked him the question: "Is it true that there are a considerable number of slaves who would prefer to remain in their present condition to becoming free?"

" Nebber see any such niggers, Massa," he answered, shaking his head decisively.. " We all want to be free. My old massa treated me kindly, but I'd a left him any minute to be my own man."

I hope the time will soon come, when, from Canada to the Gulf, there will not be a single black who is not his own man. We in the army are doing what we can, but we must be backed up by those who stay at home. My own feeling is that slavery has received its death-blow. It may continue to live for some years, but it has fallen from its pomp and pride of place. It is tottering to its fall. What shall be done with the negroes in the transition state will be a problem for statesmen to consider. I don't think we need fear the consequences of doing right, and on this subject there can be no doubt of what is right. The apparent insensibility and brutish ignorance which we find among some of the slaves will wear away under happier influences.

There is a little fellow of perhaps a dozen years who comes into our camp and runs of errands and does little services for the men. Yesterday morning he came to my tent, and with a grin, said to me, " De ol' man died last night."

" What, your father?" I inquired in surprise.

" Yes, Massa," with another grin : " Goin' to tote him off dis mornin."

As he only lived a quarter of a mile off, I got permission to go over to the house, or cabin where Scip's father had lived.

The outer door was open, and I entered without knocking. A woman was bending over a washtub at the back part of the room. I looked around me for the body but could see no indication of anything having happened out of the ordinary course.

I thought it possible that Scip had deceived me, and accordingly spoke to the woman, inquiring if she was Scip's mother.

She replied in the affirmative.

" And where is his father ?" I next inquired.

" O he 's done dead," she said, continuing her washing.

" When did he die?"

" Las' night, Massa."

" And where is the body?"

" Toted off Massa, very first t'ing dis mornin."

In spite of this case of apparent insensibility, the negro's family attachments are quite as warm naturally as our own. They have little reason, indeed, to mourn over the loss of a husband or father, since, in most cases, it is the only portal to the freedom which they covet. The separation of families, too, tends of course to weaken family ties. While I write these words I cannot help recalling our own happy home, and longing for an hour, if no more, of your society. I am glad that you find Mr. Morton so agreeable an inmate. You ought to feel quite indebted to him for his assistance in your studies. I am glad you have formed a boys' company. It is

20*

very desirable that the elements of military science should be understood even by boys, since upon them must soon devolve the defence of their country from any blows that may be directed against her, whether by foes from within or enemies from abroad.

The coming season will be a busy one with you. When you receive this letter it will be about time for you to begin to plough whatever land is to be planted. As I suggested in my first letter from camp, I should like you to devote some space — perhaps half an acre — to the culture of onions. We find them very useful for promoting health in the army. They are quite high on account of the largely increased demand, so that it will be a good crop for financial reasons.

(Here followed some directions with regard to the spring planting, which we omit, as not likely to interest our readers.) The letter ended thus : —

It is nearly time for me to mail this letter, and it is already much longer than I intended to write. May God keep you all in health and happiness is the fervent wish of

Your affectionate father,

HENRY FROST.

The intelligence that their father had been a prisoner made quite a sensation among the children. Charlie declared that Mrs. Roberts was a wicked woman, and he was glad she was put in prison — an expression of joy in which the rest fully participated.

XXVII.

POMP'S LIGHT INFANTRY TACTICS.

LITTLE Pomp continued to pursue his studies
under Frank as a teacher. By degrees his restlessness
diminished, and finding Frank firm in exacting a certain amount of study before he would dismiss him, he
concluded that it was best to study in earnest, and so
obtain the courted freedom as speedily as possible.
Frank had provided for his use a small chair, which
he had himself used when at Pomp's age, but for this
the little contraband showed no great liking. He pre-
ferred to throw himself on a rug before the open fireplace, and curling up, not unlike a cat, began to pore
over his primer.

Frank often looked up from his own studies, and
looked down with an amused glance at little Pomp's
coal-black face and glistening eyes riveted upon the
book before him. There was no lack of brightness
or intelligence in the earnest face of his young pupil.
He seemed to be studying with all his might. In a
wonderfully short time he would uncoil himself, and
coming to his teacher would say, " I guess I can say
it, Mass' Frank."

Finding how readily Pomp learned his lessons,

Frank judiciously lengthened them, so that in two
or three months, Pomp could read words of one
syllable with considerable ease, and promised very
soon to read as well as most boys of his age.

Frank also took considerable pains to cure Pomp
of his mischievous propensities, but this he found a
more difficult task than teaching him to read. Pomp
had an innate love of fun which seemed almost irre-
pressible, and his convictions of duty sat too lightly
upon him to interfere very seriously with its gratification.   One adventure into which he was led came
near having serious consequences.

Pomp, in common with other village boys of his
age, had watched with considerable interest the boys'
company, as they drilled publicly or paraded through
the main street, and he had conceived a strong
desire to get hold of a musket, to see if he too could
not go through with the manual.

Frank generally put his musket carefully away,
only bringing it out when it was needful.   One
morning, however, he had been out on a hunting
expedition, and on his return left the musket in the
corner of the shed.

Pomp espied it when he entered the house, and
resolved, if possible, to take temporary possession of
it after his lesson was over.   Having this in view,
he worked with an uncommon degree of industry,
and in less time than usual, had learned and said his
lesson.

"Very well, Pomp," said his teacher, approvingly. "You have worked unusually well to-day. If you keep on you will make quite a scholar some day."

"I'se improvin', is n't I?" inquired Pomp, with an appearance of interest.

"Yes, Pomp, you have improved rapidly. By and by you can teach your mother how to read."

"She could n't learn, Mass' Frank. She's poor ignorant nigger."

"You should n't speak so of your mother, Pomp. She's a good mother to you, and works hard to earn money to support you."

"Yes, Mass' Frank," said Pomp, who was getting impatient to go. "I guess I 'll go home and help her."

Frank thought that what he had said was producing a good effect. He did not know the secret of Pomp's haste.

Pomp left the room, and proceeding to the wood-shed, hastily possessed himself of the musket. In a stealthy manner he crept with it through a field behind the house, until he got into the neighboring woods.

He found it a hard tug to carry the gun, which was heavier than those made at the present day. At length he reached an open space in the woods, only a few rods from the road which led from the farm-house, past the shanty occupied by old Chloe. As this road was not much travelled, Pomp felt pretty safe from discovery, and accordingly here it was that he halted, and made preparations to go through the manual.

" It begins dis yer way," said Pomp, after a little reflection.

Grasping the musket with one hand he called out in an important tone : —

" 'Tention squab ! "

For the benefit of the uninitiated it may be explained that Pomp meant " Attention, squad ! "

" S'port arms ! "

Pomp found it considerably easier to give the word of command than to obey it. With some difficulty he succeeded in accomplishing this movement, and proceeded with the manual, with several original variations which would have astonished a military instructor.

Meanwhile, though Pomp did not realize it, he was exposing himself to considerably danger. The gun had been loaded with buckshot in the morning, and the charge had not been withdrawn.

It seemed to be the lot of poor Mrs. Payson to suffer fright or disaster whenever she encountered Pomp, and this memorable afternoon was to make no exception to the rule.

" Cynthy Ann," she said to her daughter, in the afternoon, " I guess I 'll go and spend the afternoon with Mis' Forbes. I haint been to see her for nigh a month, and I calc'late she 'll be glad to see me. Besides, she ginerally bakes Thursdays, an' mos likely she'll have some hot gingerbread. I'm partic'larly fond of gingerbread, an' she does know how to make it about the best of anybody I know on. You need n't wait supper for me, Cynthy Ann, for ef I don't find Mis' Forbes to home I'll go on to Mis' Frost's."

Mrs. Payson put on her cloak and hood, and armed with the workbag and the invariable blue cotton umbrella, sallied out. Mrs. Forbes lived at the distance of a mile, but Mrs. Payson was a good walker for a woman of her age, and less than half an hour brought her to the door of the brown farmhouse in which Mrs. Forbes lived.

She knocked on the door with the handle of her umbrella. The summons was answered by a girl of twelve.

"How dy do, Betsy?" said Mrs. Payson. "Is your ma'am to home?"

"No, she's gone over to Webbington to spend two or three days with aunt Prudence."

"Then she won't be home to tea," said Mrs. Payson, considerably disappointed.

"No ma'am, I don't expect her before to-morrow."

"Well, I declare for't, I am disapp'inted," said the old lady, regretfully. "I've walked a mile on puppus to see her. I'm most tuckered out."

"Won't you step in and sit down?"

"Well, I don't keer ef I do a few minutes. I

feel like to drop.   Do you do the cooking while your ma'am's gone?"

"No, she baked up enough to last before she went away."

"You haint got any gingerbread in the house?" asked Mrs. Payson, with subdued eagerness. "I always did say Mis' Forbes beat the world at makin' gingerbread."

"I'm very sorry, Mrs. Payson, but we ate the last for supper last night."

"O dear!" sighed the old lady, "I feel sort of faint, — kinder gone at the stomach.   I did n't have no appetite at dinner, and I s'pose it don't agree with me walkin' so fur on an empty stomach."

"Could n't you eat a piece of pie?" asked Betsy, sympathizingly.

"Well," said the old lady, reflectively, "I don't know but I could eat jest a bite.   But you need n't trouble yourself.   I hate to give trouble to any-body."

"O, it won't be any trouble," said Betsy, cheer-fully.

"And while you're about it," added Mrs. Payson, "ef you have got any of that cider you give me when I was here before, I don't know but I could worry down a little of it."

"Yes, we've got plenty.   I'll bring it in with the pie."

"Well," murmured the old lady, "I'll get something for my trouble. I guess I'll go and take supper at Mis' Frost's a'terwards."

Betsy brought in a slice of apple and one of pumpkin pie, and set them down before the old lady. In addition she brought a generous mug of cider.

The old lady's eyes brightened, as she saw this substantial refreshment.

"You're a good gal, Betsy," she said in the overflow of her emotions. "I was saying to my darter yesterday that I wish all the gals round her was as good and considerate as you be."

"O no, Mrs. Payson," said Betsy, modestly. "I ain't any better than girls generally."

"Yes you be. There's my granddarter Jane, ain't so respectful as she'd arter be to her old grandma'am. I often tell her that when she gets to have children of her own, she'll know what tis to be a pilgrim an' a sojourner on the arth without nobody to consider her feelin's. Your cider is putty good. (Here the old lady took a large draught, and set down the mug with a sigh of satisfaction.) It's jest the thing to take when a body's tired. It goes to the right spot. Cynthy Ann's husband did n't have none made this year. I wonder ef your ma would sell a quart or two of it."

"You can have it and welcome, Mrs Payson."

"Can I jest as well as not? Well, that's kind. But I did n't expect you to give it to me."

"O we have got plenty."

"I dunno how I can carry it home," said the old lady hesitatingly. I wonder ef some of your folks won't be going up our way within a day or two."

"We will send it. I guess father 'll be going up to-morrow."

"Then ef you can spare it you might send round a gallon, an' ef there 's anything to pay I 'll pay for 't."

This little business arrangement being satisfactorily adjusted, and the pie consumed, Mrs. Payson got up and said she must be going.

"I 'm afraid you have n't got rested yet, Mrs. Payson."

"I ain't hardly," was the reply; "but I guess 1 shall stop on the way at Mis' Frost's. Tell your ma I 'll come up an' see her ag'in afore long."

"Yes ma'am."

"An' you won't forget to send over that cider?"

"No ma'am."

"I 'm ashamed to trouble ye, but their ain't anybody over to our house that I can send. There 's Tom grudges doin' anything for his old grandma'am. A'ter all that I do for him too! Good by!"

The old lady set out on her way to Mrs. Frost's.

Her road lay through the woods, where an unforseen danger lay in wait for her.

Meanwhile, Pomp was pursuing military science under difficulties. The weight of the musket made

it very awkward for him to handle. Several times
he got out of patience with it, and apostrophized it in
terms far from complimentary. At last in one of his
awkward manœuvres, he accidentally pulled the trig-
ger. Instantly there was a loud report, followed by
a piercing shriek from the road. The charge had
entered old Mrs. Payson's umbrella and knocked it
out of her hand. The old lady fancied herself hit,
and fell backwards, kicking energetically, and
screaming " murder" at the top of her lungs.

The musket had done double execution. It was
too heavily loaded, and as it went off, ' kicked,'
leaving Pomp, about as scared as the old lady,
sprawling on the ground.

Henry Morton was only a few rods off when he
heard the explosion. He at once ran to the old
lady's assistance, fancying her hurt. She shrieked
the louder on his approach, imagining that he was
a robber, and had fired at her.

" Go away !" she cried, in affright. " I ain't got
any money. I'm a poor, destitute widder !"

" What do you take me for?" inquired Mr. Morton, somewhat amazed at this mode of address.

" Ain't you a highwayman?" asked the old lady.

" If you look at me close I think you will be able
to answer that question for yourself."

The old lady cautiously rose to a sitting posture,
and, mechanically adjusting her spectacles, took a
good look at the young man.

" Why, I declare for it, ef it ain't Mr. Morton!
I thought 't was you that fired at me."

" I hope you are not hurt," said Mr. Morton,
finding a difficulty in preserving his gravity.

" I dunno," said the old lady, dubiously, pulling
up her sleeve, and examining her arm. " I don't
see nothin ; but I expect I 've had some injury to my
innards. I feel as ef I 'd had a shock somewhere.
Do you think he 'll fire again ? " she asked, with sudden alarm.

" You need not feel alarmed," was the soothing
reply. " It was no doubt an accident."

Turning suddenly, he espied Pomp peering from
behind a tree, with eyes and mouth wide open. The
little contraband essayed a hasty flight; but Mr.
Morton, by a masterly flank movement, came upon
him, and brought forward the captive kicking and
struggling.

" Le' me go ! " said Pomp. " I ain't done noffin ! "

" Did n't you fire a gun at this lady ? "

" No," said Pomp, boldly. " Wish I may be
killed ef I did ! "

" I know 't was you — you — you imp ! " exclaimed Mrs. Payson, in violent indignation. " I
seed you do it. You 're the wust boy that ever
lived, and you 'll be hung jest as sure as I stan'
here ! "

" How did it happen, Pomp ? " asked Mr. Morton, quietly.

" It jest shooted itself ! " said Pomp, in whom the old lady's words inspired a vague feeling of alarm. " I 'clare to gracious, Mass' Morton, it did ! "

" Did n't you have the gun in your hand, Pomp? Where did you get it ? "

" I jest borrered it of Mass' Frank, to play sojer a little while," said. Pomp, reluctantly.

" Does he know that you have got it ? "

" I 'clare I done forgot to tell him," said Pomp, reluctantly.

" Will you promise never to touch it again ? "

" Don't want to ! " ejaculated Pomp, adding, spitefully, " He kick me over ! "

" I 'm glad on 't," said the old lady, emphatically, with a grim air of satisfaction. " That 'll l'arn you to fire it off at your elders ag'in. I 've a great mind to box your ears, and sarve you right, too."

Mrs. Payson advanced, to effect her purpose ; but Pomp was wary, and, adroitly freeing himself from Mr. Morton's grasp, butted at the old lady with such force that she would have fallen backwards but for the timely assistance of Mr. Morton, who sprang to her side. Her bag fell to the ground, and she struggled to regain her lost breath.

" Oh ! " groaned the old lady, gasping for breath, " he 's mos' knocked the breath out of me. I sha n't live long a'ter such a shock. I 'm achin' all over. Why did you let him do it ? "

21*

" He was too quick for me, Mrs. Payson. I hope
you feel better."

" I dunno as I shall ever feel any better," said
Mrs. Payson, gloomily. " If Cynthy Ann only
knew how her poor old ma'am had been treated !
I dunno as I shall live to get home ! "

" O yes you will," said the young man, cheerfully. " and live to see a good many years more.
Would you like to have me attend you home ? "

" I ain't got strength to go so fur," said Mrs.
Payson, who had not given up her plan of taking
tea out. " I guess I could get as fur as Mis'
Frost's, an' mebbe some on you will tackle up an'
carry me back to Cynthy Ann's a'ter tea."

Arrived at the farm-house, Mrs. Payson indulged
in a long detail of grievances ; but it was observed
that they did not materially affect her appetite at tea.

The offending musket was found by Frank under
a tree, where Pomp had dropped it when it went off.

XXVIII.

JOHN HAYNES HAS A NARROW ESCAPE.

JOHN HAYNES found the time hang heavily upon his hands after his withdrawal from the boys volunteer company. All the boys with whom he had been accustomed to associate belonged to it, and in their interest could talk of nothing else. To him, on the contrary, it was a disagreeable subject. In the pleasant spring days the company came out twice a week, and went through company drill on the Common, under the command of Frank, or Captain Frost, as he was now called.

Had Frank shown himself incompetent, and made himself ridiculous by blunders, it would have afforded John satisfaction. But Frank, thorough in all things, had so carefully prepared himself for his duties that he never made a mistake, and always acquitted himself so creditably and with such entire self-possession, that his praises were in every mouth.

Dick Bumstead, too, manifested an ambition to fill his second lieutenancy, to which, so much to his own surprise he had been elected, in such a manner as to justify the Company in their choice. In this he fully succeeded. He had become quite a different boy from what he was when we first made his acquaintance. He had learned to respect himself, and perceived with great satisfaction that he was generally respected by the boys. He no longer attempted to shirk his work in the shop, and his father now spoke of him with complacency, instead of complaint as formerly.

" Yes," said he one day, " Dick's a good boy. He was always smart, but rather fly-a-way. I could n't place any dependence upon him once, but it is not so now. I could n't wish for a better boy. I don't know what has come over him, but I hope it 'll last."

Dick happened to overhear his father speaking thus to a neighbor, and he inly determined with a commendable feeling of pride, that the change that had given his father so much pleasure should last. It does a boy good to know that his efforts are appreciated. In this case it had a happy effect upon Dick, who, I am glad to say, kept his resolution.

It has been mentioned that John was the possessor of a boat. Finding one great source of amusement cut off, and being left very much to himself, he fell back upon this, and nearly every pleasant afternoon he might be seen rowing on the river above the dam. He was obliged to confine himself to this part of the river, since, in the part below the dam, the water was too shallow.

There is one great drawback, however, upon the pleasure of owning a row-boat. It is tiresome to row single-handed after a time. So John found it, and not being over fond of active exertion he was beginning to get weary of this kind of amusement when all at once a new plan was suggested to him. This was, to rig up a mast and sail, and thus obviate the necessity of rowing.

No sooner had this plan suggested itself than he hastened to put it into execution. His boat was large enough to bear a small mast, so there was no difficulty on that head. He engaged the village carpenter to effect the desired change. He did not choose to consult his father on the subject, fearing that he might make some objection either on score of safety or expense, while he had made up his mind to have his own way.

When it was finished, and the boat with its slender mast and white sail floated gently on the quiet bosom of the stream, John's satisfaction was unbounded.

" You've got a pretty boat," said Mr. Plane, the carpenter. I suppose you know how to manage it?" he added, inquiringly.

" Yes," answered John, carelessly, " I've been in a sail-boat before to-day."

Mr. Plane's doubts were set at rest by John's confident manner, and he suppressed the caution which he had intended to give him. It made little difference, however, for John was headstrong, and would have been pretty certain to disregard whatever he might say.

It was true that this was not the first time John had been in a sail-boat; but if not the first, it was only the second. The first occasion had been three years previous, and at that time he had had nothing to do with the management of the boat, — a very important matter. It was in John's nature to be over confident, and he thought he understood merely from observation exactly how a boat ought to be managed. As we shall see, he found out his mistake.

The first day after his boat was ready John was greatly disappointed that there was no wind. The next day, as if to make up for it, the wind was very strong. Had John possessed a particle of prudence he would have seen that it was no day to venture out in a sail-boat. But he was not in the habit of curbing his impatience, and he determined that he would not wait till another day. He decided that it was a mere " capful of wind," and would be all the better for the purpose.

" It's a tip-top wind. Won't it make my boat scud; " he said to himself exultantly, as he took his place, and pushed off from shore.

Henry Morton had been out on a walk, and from the summit of a little hill near the river-bank espied John pushing off in his boat.

" He'll be sure to capsize," thought the young man in alarm. " Even if he is used to a sail-boat he is very imprudent to put out in such a wind; I will hurry down and save him if I can."

He hurried to the bank of the river, reaching it out of breath.

John was by this time some distance out. The wind had carried him along finely, the boat scudding, as he expressed it. He was congratulating himself on the success of his trial trip, when all at once a flaw struck the boat. Not being a skilful boatman he was wholly unprepared for it, and the boat upset.

Struggling in terror and confusion, John struck out for the shore. But he was not much of a swimmer, and the suddenness of the accident had unnerved him, and deprived him of his self-possession. The current of the river was rapid, and he would inevitably have drowned but for the opportune assistance of Mr. Morton.

The young man had no sooner seen the boat capsize, than he flung off his coat and boots, and, plunging into the river, swam vigorously towards the imperilled boy.

Luckily for John, Mr. Morton was, though of slight frame, muscular, and an admirable swimmer. He reached him just as John's strokes were becoming feebler and feebler; he was about to give up his unequal struggle with the waves.

"Take hold of me," he said. "Have courage, and I will save you."

John seized him with the firm grip of a drowning

person, and nearly prevented him from striking out.
But Mr. Morton's strength served him in good stead;
and, notwithstanding the heavy burden, he succeeded
in reaching the bank in safety, though with much
exhaustion.

John no sooner reached the bank than he fainted
away. The great danger which he had just escaped,
added to his own efforts, had proved too much for
him.

Mr. Morton, fortunately, knew how to act in such
emergencies. By the use of the proper remedies,
he was fortunately brought to himself, and his preserver offered to accompany him home. John still
felt giddy, and was glad to accept Mr. Morton's
offer. He knew that his father would be angry with
him for having the boat fitted up without his knowledge, especially as he had directed Mr. Plane to
charge it to his father's account. Supposing that
Squire Haynes approved, the carpenter made no objections to doing so. But even the apprehension of
his father's anger was swallowed up by the thought
of the great peril from which he had just escaped,
and the discomfort of the wet clothes which he had
on.

Mr. Morton, too, was completely wet through,
with the exception of his coat, and but for John's
apparent inability to go home alone, would at once
have returned to his boarding-place to exchange his
wet clothes for dry ones.

It so happened that Squire Haynes was sitting at a front window, and saw Mr. Morton and his son as they entered the gate and came up the gravelled walk. He had never met Mr. Morton, and was surprised now at seeing him in John's company. He had conceived a feeling of dislike to the young man, for which he could not account, while at the same time he felt a strong curiosity to know more of him.

When they came nearer, he perceived the drenched garments, and went to the door himself to admit them.

" What 's the matter, John ? " he demanded, hastily, with a contraction of the eyebrows.

" I 'm wet ! " said John, shortly.

" It is easy to see that. But how came you so wet ? "

" I 've been in the river," answered John, who did not seem disposed to volunteer any particulars of his adventure.

" How came you there ? "

" Your son's boat capsized," explained Mr. Morton ; " and, as you will judge from my appearance, I jumped in after him. I should advise him to change his clothing, or he will be likely to take cold."

Squire Haynes looked puzzled.

" I don't see how a large row-boat like his could capsize," he said ; " he must have been very careless."

22

"It was a sail-boat," explained John, rather reluctantly.

"A sail-boat! Whose?"

"Mine."

"I don't understand at all."

"I had a mast put in, and a sail rigged up, two or three days since," said John, compelled at last to explain.

"Why did you do this without my permission?" demanded the Squire, angrily.

"Perhaps," said Mr. Morton, quietly, "it will be better to postpone inquiries until your son has changed his clothes.

Squire Haynes, though somewhat irritated by this interference, bethought himself that it would be churlish not to thank his son's preserver.

"I am indebted to you, sir," he said, "for your agency in saving the life of this rash boy. I regret that you should have got wet."

"I shall probably experience nothing more than temporary inconvenience."

"You have been some months in the village, I believe, Mr. Morton. I trust you will call at an early day, and enable me to follow up the chance which has made us acquainted."

"I seldom make calls," said Mr. Morton, in a distant tone. "Yet," added he, after a pause, "I may have occasion to accept your invitation some day. Good morning, sir."

"Good morning," returned the Squire, looking after him with an expression of perplexity.

"He boards at the Frosts', does n't he, John?" asked Squire Haynes, turning to his son.

"Yes, sir."

"There's something in his face that seems familiar," mused the Squire, absently. "He reminds me of somebody, though I can't recall who."

It was not long before the Squire's memory was refreshed, and he obtained clearer information respecting the young man, and the errand which had brought him to Rossville. When that information came, it was so far from pleasing that he would willingly have postponed it indefinitely.

XXIX.

THE planting season was over. For a month Frank had worked industriously, in conjunction with Jacob Carter. His father had sent him directions so full and minute, that he was not often obliged to call upon Farmer Maynard for advice. The old farmer proved to be very kind and obliging. Jacob, too, was capable and faithful, so that the farm work went on as well probably as if Mr. Frost had been at home.

One evening towards the middle of June, Frank walked out into the fields with Mr. Morton. The corn and potatoes were looking finely. The garden vegetables were up, and to all appearance doing well. Frank surveyed the scene with a feeling of natural pride.

"Don't you think I would make a successful farmer, Mr. Morton?" he asked.

"Yes, Frank; and more than this, I think you will be likely to succeed in any other vocation you may select."

"I am afraid you are flattering me, Mr. Morton."

"Such is not my intention, Frank, but I like to award praise where I think it due. I have noticed in you a disposition to be faithful to whatever responsibility is imposed upon you, and wherever I see that I feel no hesitation in predicting a successful career."

"Thank you," said Frank, looking very much pleased with the compliment. "I try to be faithful. I feel that father has trusted me more than it is usual to trust boys of my age, and I want to show myself worthy of his confidence."

"You are fortunate in having a father, Frank," said the young man, with a shade of sadness in his voice. "My father died before I was of your age."

"Do you remember him?" inquired Frank, with interest.

"I remember him well. He was always kind to me. I never remember to have received a harsh word from him. It is because he was so kind and indulgent to me that I feel the more incensed against a man who took advantage of his confidence to defraud him, or rather me, through him."

"You have never mentioned this before, Mr. Morton."

"No. I have left you all in ignorance of much of my history. This morning, if it will interest you, I propose to take you into my confidence."

The eagerness with which Frank greeted this proposal showed that for him the story would have no lack of interest.

22*

"Let us sit down under this tree," said Henry Morton, pointing to a horse-chestnut, whose dense foliage promised a pleasant shelter from the sun's rays.

They threw themselves upon the grass, and he forthwith commenced his story.

"My father was born in Boston, and growing up engaged in mercantile pursuits. He was moderately successful, and finally accumulated fifty thousand dollars. He would not have stopped there, for he was at the time making money rapidly, but his health became precarious, and his physician required him absolutely to give up business. The seeds of consumption, which probably had been lurking for years in his system, had begun to show themselves unmistakably, and required immediate attention.

"By the advice of his physician he sailed for the West India Islands, hoping that the climate might have a beneficial effect upon him. At that time I was twelve years old, and an only child. My mother had died some years before, so that I was left quite alone in the world. I was sent for a time to Virginia, to my mother's brother, who possessed a large plantation and numerous slaves. Here I remained for six months. You will remember that Aunt Chloe recognized me at first sight. You will not be surprised at this when I tell you that she was my uncle's slave, and that as a boy I was indebted to her for many a little favor which she, being employed in the kitchen, was able to render me. As I told you at the

time, my real name is not Morton. It will not be
long before you understand the reason of my con-
cealment.

" My father had a legal adviser, in whom he reposed a large measure of confidence, though events
showed him to be quite unworthy of it. On leaving
Boston he divided his property, which had been con-
verted into money, into two equal portions. One
part he took with him. The other he committed to
the lawyer's charge. So much confidence had he in
this man's honor, that he did not even require a receipt. One additional safeguard he had, however.
This was the evidence of the lawyer's clerk, who
was present on the occasion of the deposit.

" My father went to the West Indies, but the
change seemed only to accelerate the progress of his
malady. He lingered for a few months and then
died. Before his death he wrote two letters, one to
my uncle and one to myself. In these he communi-
cated the fact of his having deposited twenty-five
thousand dollars with his lawyer. He mentioned
incidentally the presence of the lawyer's clerk at the
time. I am a little surprised that he should have
done it, as not the faintest suspicion of the lawyer's
good faith had entered his thoughts.

" On receiving this letter my uncle, on my behalf,
took measures to claim this sum, and for this purpose
came to Boston. Imagine his surprise and indignation when the lawyer positively denied having re-

ceived any such deposit, and called upon him to prove
it. With great effrontery he declared that it was
absurd to suppose that my father would have entrust-
ed him with any such sum without a receipt for it.
This certainly looked plausible, and I acknowledge
that few except my father, who never trusted without
trusting entirely, would have acted so imprudently.

"'Where is the clerk who was in your office at
the time?' inquired my uncle.

"The lawyer looked somewhat discomposed at
this question.

"'Why do you ask,' he inquired, abruptly.

"'Because,' was the reply, 'his evidence is very
important to us. My brother states that he was
present when the deposit was made.'

"'I don't know where he is,' said the lawyer.
'He was too dissipated to remain in my office, and
I accordingly discharged him.'

"My uncle suspected that the clerk had been
bribed to keep silence, and for additional security
sent off to some distant place.

"Nothing could be done. Strong as were our
suspicions, and absolute as was our conviction of the
lawyer's guilt, we had no resource. But from that
time I devoted my life to the exposure of this man.
Fortunately I was not without means. The other
half of my father's property came to me; and the
interest being considerably more than I required for
my support, I have devoted the remainder to prose-

cuting inquiries respecting the missing clerk. Just
before I came to Rossville, I obtained a clew which I
have since industriously followed up.

"Last night I received a letter from my agent,
stating that he had found the man, — that he was in
a sad state of destitution, and that he was ready to
give his evidence."

"Is the lawyer still living?" inquired Frank,
eagerly.

"He is."

"What a villain he must be."

"I am afraid he is, Frank."

"Does he still live in Boston?"

"No. After he had made sure of his ill-gotten
gains, he removed into the country, where he built
him a fine house. He has been able to live a life of
leisure; but I doubt if he has been as happy as he
would have been had he never deviated from the path
of rectitude."

"Have you seen him lately?" asked Frank.

"I have seen him many times within the last few
months," said the young man, in a significant tone.

Frank jumped to his feet in surprise. "You
don't mean—" he said, as a sudden suspicion of the
truth dawned upon his mind.

"Yes," said Mr. Morton, deliberately, "I do
mean that the lawyer who defrauded my father lives
in this village. You know him well as Squire
Haynes."

"I can hardly believe it," said Frank, unable to conceal his astonishment. "Do you think he knows who you are?"

"I think he has noticed my resemblance to my father. If I had not assumed a different name he would have been sure to detect me. This would have interfered with my plans, as he undoubtedly knew the whereabouts of his old clerk, and would have arranged to remove him, so as to delay his discovery, perhaps indefinitely. Here is the letter I received last night. I will read it to you."

The letter ran as follows : —

"I have at length discovered the man of whom I have so long been in search. I found him in Detroit. He had recently removed thither from St. Louis. He is very poor, and when I found him was laid up with typhoid fever in a mean lodging-house. I removed him to more comfortable quarters, supplied him with relishing food and good medical assistance. Otherwise I think he would have died. The result is, that he feels deeply grateful to me for having probably saved his life. When I first broached the idea of his giving evidence against his old employer, I found him reluctant to do so, — not from any attachment he bore him, but from a fear that he would be held on a criminal charge for concealing a felony. I have undertaken to assure him, on your behalf, that he shall not be punished if he will come forward and give his evidence unhesitat-

ingly.   I have finally obtained his promise to do
so.

"We shall leave Detroit day after to-morrow, and
proceed to New England by way of New York.
Can you meet me in New York on the 18th inst.?
You can, in that case, have an interview with this
man, Travers; and it will be well to obtain his confession, legally certified, to guard against any vacil-
lation of purpose on his part.   I have no apprehension of it, but it is as well to be certain."

This letter was signed by Mr. Morton's agent.

"I was very glad to get that letter, Frank," said
his companion.   "I don't think I care so much for
the money, though that is not to be despised, since
it will enable me to do more good than at present I
have it in my power to do.   But there is one thing
I care for still more, and that is, to redeem my
father's memory from reproach.   In the last letter
he ever wrote he made a specific statement, which
this lawyer declares to be false.   The evidence of his
clerk will hurl back the falsehood upon himself."

"How strange it is, Mr. Morton," exclaimed
Frank, "that you should have saved the life of a
son of the man who has done so much to injure
you!"

"Yes, that gives me great satisfaction.   I do not
wish Squire Haynes any harm, but I am determined
that justice shall be done.   Otherwise than that, if I
can be of any service to him, I shall not refuse."

"I remember now," said Frank, after a moment's pause, "that on the first Sunday you appeared at church, Squire Haynes stopped me to inquire who you were."

"I am thought to look much as my father did. He undoubtedly saw the resemblance. I have often caught his eyes fixed upon me in perplexity when he did not know that I noticed him. It is fourteen years since my father died. Retribution has been slow, but it has come at last."

"When do you go on to New York?" asked Frank, recalling the agent's request.

"I shall start to-morrow morning. For the present I will ask you to keep what I have said a secret even from your good mother. It is as well not to disturb Squire Haynes in his fancied security until we are ready to overwhelm him with our evidence."

"How long shall you be absent, Mr. Morton?"

"Probably less than a week. I shall merely say that I have gone on business. I trust to your discretion to say nothing more."

"I certainly will not," said Frank. "I am very much obliged to you for having told me first."

The two rose from their grassy seats, and walked slowly back to the farm-house.

XXX.

THE next morning Mr. Morton was a passenger by the early stage for Webbington, where he took the train for Boston. Thence he was to proceed to New York by the steamboat train.

"Good by, Mr. Morton," said Frank, waving his cap as the stage started. "I hope you'll soon be back."

"I hope so too; good by."

Crack went the whip, round went the wheels. The horses started, and the stage rumbled off, swaying this way and that, as if top-heavy.

Frank went slowly back to the house, feeling quite lonely. He had become so accustomed to Mr. Morton's companionship that his departure left a void which he hardly knew how to fill.

As he reflected upon Mr. Morton's story he began to feel an increased uneasiness at the mortgage held by Squire Haynes upon his father's farm. The time was very near at hand — only ten days off — when the mortgage might be foreclosed, and but half the money was in readiness.

Perhaps, however, Squire Haynes had no intention of foreclosing. If so, there was no occasion for

23

apprehension. But about this he felt by no means certain.

He finally determined, without consulting his mother, to make the Squire a visit and inquire frankly what he intended to do. The Squire's answer would regulate his future proceedings.

It was Frank's rule — and a very good one too — to do at once whatever needed to be done. He resolved to lose no time in making his call.

" Frank," said his mother, as he entered the house, " I want you to go down to the store some time this forenoon, and get me half a dozen pounds of sugar."

" Very well, mother, I'll go now. I suppose it won't make any difference if I don't come back for an hour or two."

" No, that will be in time."

Mrs. Frost did not ask Frank where he was going. She had perfect faith in him, and felt sure that he would never become involved in anything discreditable.

Frank passed through the village without stopping at the store. He deferred his mother's errand until his return. Passing up the village street, he stopped before the fine house of Squire Haynes. Opening the gate he walked up the gravelled path and rang the bell.

A servant-girl came to the door.

" Is Squire Haynes at home?" inquired Frank.

" Yes, but he's eating breakfast."

"Will he be through soon?"

"Shure and I think so."

"Then I will step in and wait for him."

"Who shall I say it is?"

"Frank Frost."

Squire Haynes had just passed his cup for coffee when Bridget entered and reported that Frank Frost was in the drawing-room and would like to see him when he had finished his breakfast.

"Frank Frost!" repeated the Squire, arching his eyebrows. "What does he want, I wonder?"

"Shure he did n't say," said Bridget.

"Very well."

"He is Captain of the boys' company, John, is n't he?" asked the Squire.

"Yes," said John, sulkily. "I wish him joy of his office. I would n't have anything to do with such a crowd of ragamuffins."

Of course the reader understands that this was "sour grapes" on John's part.

Finishing his breakfast leisurely, Squire Haynes went into the room where Frank was sitting patiently awaiting him.

Frank rose as he entered.

"Good morning, Squire Haynes," he said, politely rising as he spoke.

"Good morning," said the Squire, coldly. "You are an early visitor."

If this was intended for a rebuff, Frank did not choose to take any notice of it.

"I call on a little matter of business, Squire Haynes," continued Frank.

"Very well," said the Squire, seating himself in a luxurious arm-chair, "I am ready to attend to you."

"I believe you hold a mortgage on our farm."

Squire Haynes started. The thought of Frank's real business had not occurred to him. He had hoped that nothing would have been said in relation to the mortgage until he was at liberty to foreclose, as he wished to take the Frosts unprepared. He now resolved, if possible, to keep Frank in ignorance of his real purpose, that he might not think it necessary to prepare for his attack.

"Yes," said he, indifferently; "I hold quite a number of mortgages, and one upon your father's farm among them."

"Isn't the time nearly run out?" asked Frank, anxiously.

"I can look if you desire it," said the Squire, in the same indifferent tone.

"I should be glad if you would."

"May I ask why you are desirous of ascertaining the precise date?" asked the Squire. "Are you intending to pay off the mortgage?"

"No sir," said Frank. "We are not prepared to do so at present."

Squire Haynes felt relieved. He feared for a moment that Mr. Frost had secured the necessary sum, and that he would be defeated in his wicked purpose.

He drew out a large number of papers, which he rather ostentatiously scattered about the table, and finally came to the mortgage.

"The mortgage comes due on the first of July," he said.

"Will it be convenient for you to renew it, Squire Haynes?" asked Frank, anxiously. "Father being absent, it would be inconvenient for us to obtain the amount necessary to cancel it. Of course I shall be ready to pay the interest promptly."

"Unless I should have sudden occasion for the money," said the Squire, "I will let it remain. I don't think you need feel any anxiety on the subject."

With the intention of putting Frank off his guard, Squire Haynes assumed a comparatively gracious tone. This, in the case of any other man, would have completely reassured Frank. But he had a strong distrust of the Squire, since the revelation of his character made by his friend Mr. Morton.

"Could you tell me positively?" he asked, still uneasy. "It is only ten days now to the first of July, and that is little enough to raise the money in."

"Don't trouble yourself," said the Squire. "I said unless I had sudden occasion for the money, because unforeseen circumstances might arise. But as I have a considerable sum lying at the bank, I don't anticipate anything of the kind."

23*

"I suppose you will give me immediate notice, should it be necessary. We can pay four hundred dollars now. So, if you please, the new mortgage can be made out for half the present amount."

"Very well," said the Squire, carelessly. "Just as you please as to that. Still, as you have always paid me interest regularly, I consider the investment a good one, and have no objection to the whole remaining."

"Thank you, sir," said Frank, rising to go.

Frank took his hat, and bowing to the Squire, sought the front door. His face wore a perplexed expression. He hardly knew what to think about the interview he had just had.

"Squire Haynes talks fair enough," he soliloquized; "and perhaps he means what he says. If it hadn't been for what Mr. Morton told me, I should have confidence in him. But a man who will betray a trust is capable of breaking his word to me. I think I'll look round a little, and see if I can't provide for the worst in case it comes."

Just after Frank left the house, John entered his father's presence.

"What did Frank Frost want of you, father?" he asked.

"He came about the mortgage."

"Did he want to pay it?"

"No, he wants me to renew it."

" Of course you refused."

" Of course I did no such thing. Do you think I am a fool?"

" You don't mean to say that you agreed to renew it?" demanded John, in angry amazement.

Squire Haynes rather enjoyed John's mystification.

" Come," said he, " I'm afraid you'll never make a lawyer if you're not sharper than that comes to. Never reveal your plans to your adversary. That's an important principle. If I had refused, he would have gone to work, and in the ten days between now and the first of July, he'd have managed in some way to scrape together the eight hundred dollars. He's got half of it now."

" What did you tell him, then?"

" I put him off by telling him not to trouble himself, — that I would not foreclose the mortgage unless I had unexpected occasion for the money."

" Yes, I see," said John, his face brightening at the anticipated disaster to the Frosts. " You'll take care that there shall be some sudden occasion."

" Yes," said the Squire, complacently. " I'll have a note come due, which I had not thought about, or something of the kind."

" O, that'll be bully."

" Don't use such low words, John. I have repeatedly requested you to be more careful about your language. By the way, your teacher told me yesterday that you are not doing as well now as formerly."

" O, he 's an old muff. Besides, he 's got a spite
against me. I should do a good deal better at
another school."

" We 'll see about that.   But I suspect he 's partly
right."

" Well, how can a feller study when he knows
the teacher is determined to be down upon him ? "

" ' Feller ! ' I am shocked at hearing you use that
word.   ' Down upon him,' too ! "

" Very well ; let me go where I won't hear such
language spoken."

It would have been well if Squire Haynes had
been as much shocked by bad actions as by low
language.

This little disagreement over, they began again to
anticipate with pleasure the effect of the Squire's
premeditated blow upon the Frosts.

" We 'll come up with 'em ? " said John, with inward exultation.

Meanwhile, though the Squire was entirely unconscious of it, there was a sword hanging over his
own head.

XXXI.

SQUIRE HAYNES SPRINGS HIS TRAP.

As intimated in the last chapter, Frank determined to see if he could not raise the money necessary to pay off the mortgage in case it should be necessary to do so.

Farmer Maynard was a man in very good circumstances. He owned an excellent farm, which yielded more than enough to support his family. Probably he had one or two thousand dollars laid aside.

"I think he will help me," Frank said to himself, "I'll go to him."

He went to the house, and was directed to the barn. There he found the farmer engaged in mending a hoe-handle, which had been broken, by splicing it.

He unfolded his business. The farmer listened attentively to his statement.

"You say the Squire as much as told you that he would renew the mortgage?"

"Yes."

"Well, I wouldn't trouble myself then; I've no doubt he'll do it."

"He said, unless he should have some sudden occasion for the money."

"All right. He is a prudent man, and don't want to bind himself. That is all. You know the most unlikely things may happen; but I don't believe the Squire 'll want the money. He 's got plenty in the bank."

"But if he should?"

"Then he 'll wait, or take part. I suppose you can pay part."

"Yes, half."

"Then I guess there won't be any chance of anything going wrong."

"If there should," persisted Frank, "could you lend us four hundred dollars to make up the amount?"

"I 'd do it in a minute, Frank, but I haint got the money by me. What money I have got besides the farm is lent out in notes. Only last week I let my brother-in-law have five hundred dollars, and that leaves me pretty short."

"Perhaps somebody else will advance the money," said Frank, feeling a little discouraged at the result of his first application.

"Yes, most likely. But I guess you won't need any assistance. I look upon it as certain that the mortgage will be renewed. Next fall I shall have the money, and if the Squire wants to dispose of the mortgage, I shall be ready to take it off his hands."

Frank tried to feel that he was foolish in appre-
hending trouble from Squire Haynes, but he found it
impossible to rid himself of a vague feeling of uneasiness.

He made application to another farmer — an intimate friend of his father's — but he had just purchased and paid for a five-acre lot adjoining his farm,
and that had stripped him of money. He too bade
Frank lay aside all anxiety, and assured him that his
fears were groundless.

With this Frank had to be content.

"Perhaps I am foolish," he said to himself. "I'll
try to think no more about it."

He accordingly returned to his usual work, and
not wishing to trouble his mother to no purpose, resolved not to impart his fears to her. Another
ground of relief suggested itself to him. Mr.
Morton would probably be back on the 27th of
June. Such at least was his anticipation when he
went away. There was reason to believe that he
would be both ready and willing to take up the
mortgage, if needful. This thought brought back
Frank's cheerfulness.

It was somewhat dashed by the following letter
which he received a day or two later from his absent
friend. It was dated New York, June 25, 1863.
As will appear from its tenor, it prepared Frank for
a further delay in Mr. Morton's arrival.

Dear Frank : —

I shall not be able to be with you quite as soon as I intended. I hope, however, to return a day or two afterwards at latest. My business is going on well, and I am assured of final success. Will you ask your mother if she can accommodate an acquaintance of mine for a day or two? I shall bring him with me from New York, and shall feel indebted for the accommodation.

Your true friend,
HENRY MORTON.

Frank understood at once that the acquaintance referred to must be the clerk, whose evidence was so important to Mr. Morton's case. Being enjoined to secrecy, however, he of course felt that he was not at liberty to mention this.

One day succeeded another until at length the morning of the thirtieth of June dawned. Mr. Morton had not yet arrived; but, on the other hand, nothing had been heard from Squire Haynes.

Frank began to breathe more freely. He persuaded himself that he had been foolishly apprehensive. "The Squire means to renew the mortgage," he said to himself, hopefully.

He had a talk with his mother, and she agreed that it would be well to pay the four hundred dollars they could spare, and have a new mortgage made out for the balance. Frank accordingly rode over to Brandon in the forenoon, and withdrew from the bank the entire sum there deposited to his father's credit. This, with money which had been received from Mr. Morton in payment of his board, made up the requisite amount.

About four o'clock in the afternoon, as Mrs. Frost was sewing at a front window, she exclaimed to Frank, who was making a kite for his little brother Charlie, " Frank, there's Squire Haynes coming up the road."

Frank's heart gave an anxious bound.

" Is he coming here?" he asked, with anxiety.

" Yes," said Mrs. Frost, after a moment's pause.

Frank turned pale with apprehension.

A moment afterwards the huge knocker was heard to sound, and Mrs. Frost, putting down her work, smoothed her apron and went to the door.

" Good afternoon, Mrs. Frost," said the Squire, lifting his hat.

" Good afternoon, Squire Haynes. Won't you walk in?"

" Thank you; I will intrude for a few minutes. How do you do?" he said, nodding to Frank as he entered.

" Pretty well, thank you, sir," said Frank, nervously.

The Squire, knowing the odium which would attach to the course he had settled upon, resolved to show the utmost politeness to the family he was

24

about to injure, and justify his action by the plea of necessity.

"Take a seat, Squire Haynes," said Mrs. Frost. "You'll find this rocking-chair more comfortable."

"I am very well seated, thank you. I cannot stop long. I have merely called on a matter of business."

"About the mortgage?" interrupted Frank, who could keep silence no longer.

"Precisely so. I regret to say that I have urgent occasion for the money, and shall be unable to renew it."

"We have got four hundred dollars," said Mrs. Frost, "which we are intending to pay."

"I am sorry to say that this will not answer my purpose."

"Why did you not let us know before?" asked Frank, abruptly.

"Frank!" said his mother, reprovingly.

"It was only this morning that the necessity arose. I have a note due which must be paid."

"We are not provided with the money, Squire Haynes," said Mrs. Frost. "If, however, you will wait a few days, we can probably raise it among our friends."

"I regret to say that this will not do," said the Squire. "I would gladly postpone the matter. The investment has been satisfactory to me, but necessity knows no law."

Frank was about to burst out with some indignant exclamation, but his mother, checking him, said: "I think there is little chance of our being able to pay you to-morrow. May I inquire what course you propose to take?"

"It will be my painful duty to foreclose the mortgage."

"Squire Haynes," said Frank, boldly, "haven't you intended to foreclose the mortgage all along? Hadn't you decided about it when I called upon you ten days ago?"

"What do you mean by your impertinence, sir?" demanded the Squire, giving vent to his anger.

"Just what I say. I believe you bear a grudge against my father, and only put me off the other day in order to prevent my being able to meet your demands to-morrow. What do you suppose we can do in less than twenty-four hours?"

"Madam!" said the Squire, purple with rage, "do you permit your son to insult me in this manner?"

"I leave it to your own conscience, Squire Haynes, whether his charges are not deserved. I do not like to think ill of any man, but your course is very suspicious."

"Madam," said Squire Haynes, now thoroughly enraged, "you are a woman, and can say what you please; but as for this young rascal, I'll beat him within an inch of his life if ever I catch him out of your presence."

"He is under the protection of the laws," said Mrs. Frost, composedly, "which you, being a lawyer, ought to understand."

"I'll have no mercy on you.   I'll sell you up root and branch," said Squire Haynes, trembling with passion, and smiting the floor with his cane.

"At all events the house is ours to-day," returned Mrs. Frost, with dignity, "and I must request you to leave us in quiet possession of it."

The Squire left the house in undignified haste, muttering threats as he went.

"Good, mother!" exclaimed Frank, admiringly. "You turned him out capitally.   But," he added, an expression of dismay stealing over his face, "what shall we do ?"

"We must try to obtain a loan," said Mrs. Frost, "I will go and see Mr. Sanger, while you go to Mr. Perry.   Possibly they may help us.   There is no time to be lost."

An hour afterwards Frank and his mother returned, both disappointed.   Mr. Sanger and Mr. Perry both had the will to help but not the ability.   There seemed no hope left save in Mr. Morton.

At six o'clock the stage rumbled up to the gate.

"Thank heaven! Mr. Morton has come!" exclaimed Frank, eagerly.

Mr. Morton got out of the stage, and with him a feeble old man, or such he seemed, whom the young man assisted to alight.   They came up the gravel walk together.

" How do you do, Frank ? " he said, with a cheerful smile.

" We are in trouble," said Frank. " Squire
Haynes is going to foreclose the mortgage to-
morrow."

" Never mind ! " said Mr. Morton. " We will be
ready for him. He can't do either of us any more
mischief, Frank. His race is about run."

A heavy weight seemed lifted from Frank's heart.
For the rest of the day he was in wild spirits. He
asked no questions of Mr. Morton. He felt a firm
confidence that all would turn out for the best.

24*

XXXII.

TURNING THE TABLES.

THE next morning Mr. Morton made inquiries of Frank respecting the mortgage. Frank explained that a loan of four hundred dollars would enable him to cancel it.

"That is very easily arranged then," said Henry Morton.

He opened his pocket-book and drew out four crisp new United States notes, of one hundred dollars each.

"There, Frank," said he; "that will loosen the hold Squire Haynes has upon you. I fancy he will find it a little more difficult to extricate himself from my grasp."

"How can I ever thank you, Mr. Morton?" said Frank with emotion.

"It gives me great pleasure to have it in my power to be of service to you, Frank," said his friend kindly.

"We will have a mortgage made out to you," continued Frank.

"Not without my consent, I hope," said Mr. Morton, smiling.

Frank looked puzzled.

" No, Frank," resumed Mr. Morton, " I don't care for any security. You may give me a simple acknowledgment of indebtedness, and then pay me at your leisure."

Frank felt with justice that Mr. Morton was acting very generously, and he was more than ever drawn to him.

So passed the earlier hours of the forenoon.

About eleven o'clock Squire Haynes was observed approaching the house. His step was firm and elastic, as if he rejoiced in the errand he was upon. Again he lifted the knocker, and sounded a noisy summons. It was in reality a summons to surrender.

The door was opened again by Mrs. Frost, who invited the Squire to enter. He did so, wondering at her apparent composure.

" They can't have raised the money," thought he, apprehensively. " No, I am sure the notice was too short."

Frank was in the room, but Squire Haynes did not deign to notice him, nor did Frank choose to make advances. Mrs. Frost spoke upon indifferent subjects, being determined to force Squire Haynes to broach himself the business that had brought him to the farm.

Finally, clearing his throat, he said : " Well, madam, are you prepared to cancel the mortgage which I hold upon your husband's farm ? "

"I hope," said Mrs. Frost, "you will give us time. It is hardly possible to obtain so large a sum in twenty-four hours."

"They have n't got it," thought the Squire, exultingly.

"As to that," he said aloud, "you 've had several years to get ready in."

"Have you no consideration? Remember my husband's absence, and that I am unacquainted with business."

"I have already told you," said the Squire, hastily, "that I require the money. I have a note to pay, and — "

"Can you give us a week?"

"No, I must have the money at once."

"And if we cannot pay?"

"I must foreclose."

"Will that give you the money any sooner? I suppose you would have to advertise the farm for sale before you could realize anything, and I hardly think that can be accomplished sooner than a week hence."

"The delay is only a subterfuge on your part," said the Squire, hotly. "You would be no better prepared at the end of a week than you are now."

"No, perhaps not;" said Mrs. Frost, quietly.

"And yet you ask me to wait," said the Squire, indignantly. "Once for all, let me tell you that all entreaties are vain. My mind is made up to foreclose, and foreclose I will."

"Don't be too sure of that," interrupted Frank, with a triumphant smile.

"Ha, young impudence!" exclaimed the Squire, wheeling round. "Who's to prevent me, I should like to know?"

"I am," said Frank, boldly.

The Squire fingered his cane nervously. He was very strongly tempted to lay it on our hero's back. But he reflected that the power was in his hands, and that he was sure of his revenge.

"You won't gain anything by your impertinence," he said, loftily. "I might have got you a place, out of pity to your mother, if you had behaved differently. I need a boy to do odd jobs about the house, and I might have offered the place to you."

"Thank you for your kind intentions," said Frank, "but I fear the care of this farm will prevent my accepting your tempting offer."

"The care of the farm!" repeated the Squire, angrily. "Do you think I will delegate it to you?"

"I don't see what you have to do about it," said Frank.

"Then you'll find out," roared the Squire. "I shall take immediate possession, and require you to leave at once."

"Then I suppose we had better pay the mortgage, mother," said Frank.

"Pay the mortgage! You can't do it," said the Squire, exultingly.

"Have you the document with you?" inquired Mrs. Frost.

"Yes, madam."

"Name the amount due on it."

"With interest eight hundred and twenty-four dollars."

"Frank, you may call in Mr. Morton as a witness."

Mr. Morton entered.

"Now Frank, you may count out the money."

"What!" stammered the Squire, in dismay, "can you pay it?"

"We can."

"Why did n't you tell me so in the first place?" demanded Squire Haynes, his wrath excited by his bitter disappointment.

"I wished to ascertain whether your course was dictated by necessity or a desire to annoy and injure us. I can have no further doubt about it."

There was no help for it. Squire Haynes was compelled to release his hold upon the Frost Farm, and pocket his money. He had never been so sorry to receive money before.

This business over, he was about to beat a hurried retreat, when he was suddenly arrested by a question from Henry Morton.

"Can you spare me a few minutes, Squire Haynes?"

"I am in haste, sir."

"My business is important, and has already been too long delayed."

" Too long delayed?"

" Yes, it has waited twelve years."

" I don't understand you, sir," said the Squire.

" Perhaps I can assist you. You know me as Henry Morton. That is not my real name."

" An *alias* !" sneered the Squire in a significant tone.

" Yes, I had my reasons," returned the young man, unmoved.

" I have no doubt of it."

Henry Morton smiled, but did not otherwise notice the unpleasant imputation.

" My real name is Richard Waring."

Squire Haynes started violently, and scrutinized the young man closely through his spectacles. His vague suspicions were confirmed.

" Do you wish to know my business with you?"

The Squire muttered something inaudible.

" I demand the restitution of the large sum of money intrusted to you by my father, just before his departure to the West Indies, — a sum of which you have been the wrongful possessor for twelve years."

" Do you mean to insult me?" exclaimed the Squire, bold in the assurance that the sole evidence of his fraud was undiscovered.

" Unless you comply with my demand I shall proceed against you legally, and you are enough of a lawyer to understand the punishment meted out to that description of felony."

"Pooh, pooh! Your threats won't avail you," said the Squire, contemptuously. "Your plan is a very clumsy one. Let me suggest to you, young man, that threats for the purpose of extorting money are actionable."

"Do you doubt my identity?"

"You may very probably be the person you claim to be, but that won't save you."

"Very well. You have conceded one point."

He walked quietly to the door of the adjoining room, opened it, and in a distinct voice called "James Travers."

At the sound of this name, Squire Haynes sank into a chair, ashy pale.

A man, not over forty, but with seamed face, hair nearly white, and a form evidently broken with ill health, slowly entered.

Squire Haynes beheld him with dismay.

"You see before you, Squire Haynes, a man whose silence has been your safeguard for the last twelve years. His lips are now unsealed. James Travers, tell us what you know of the trust reposed in this man, by my father."

"No, no," said the Squire, hurriedly. "It — it is enough. I will make restitution."

"You have done wisely," said Richard Waring. (We must give him his true name.) "When will you be ready to meet me upon this business?"

"To-morrow," muttered the Squire.

He left the house with the air of one who has been crushed by a sudden blow.

The pride of the haughty had been laid low, and retribution, long deferred, had come at last.

Numerous and hearty were the congratulations which Mr. Morton (I mean Mr. Waring) received upon his new accession of property.

" I do not care so much for that," he said ; " but my father's word has been vindicated. My mind is now at peace."

There was more than one happy heart at the farm, that night. Mr. Waring had accomplished the great object of his life ; and as for Frank and his mother, they felt that the black cloud which had menaced their happiness had been removed, and henceforth there seemed prosperous days in store. To cap the climax of their happiness, the afternoon mail brought a letter from Mr. Frost, in which he imparted the intelligence that he had been promoted to a second lieutenancy.

" Mother," said Frank, " you must be very dig-nified now. You are an officer's wife."

25

XXXIII.

THE restitution which Squire Haynes was compelled to make, stripped him of more than half his property. His mortification and chagrin were so great that he determined to remove from Rossville. He gave no intimation where he was going; but it is understood that he is now living in the vicinity of Philadelphia, in a much more modest way than at Rossville.

To anticipate matters a little, it may be said that John was recently examined for college, but failed so signally that he will not again make the attempt. He has shown a disposition to be extravagant, which, unless curbed, will help him run through his father's diminished property at a rapid rate whenever it shall come into his possession.

The Squire's handsome house in Rossville was purchased by Henry Morton (I must still be allowed to call him thus, though not his real name). He has not yet taken up his residence there, but there is reason to believe that erelong there will be a Mrs. Morton, to keep him company therein.

Not long since, as he and Frank lay stretched out beneath a thick branching oak in the front-yard at the farm, Mr. Morton turned to our hero and said, " Are you meaning to go to college when your father comes home, Frank?"

Frank hesitated.

" I have always looked forward to it," he said, " but lately I have been thinking that I shall have to give up the idea."

" Why so?"

" Because it is so expensive that my father cannot, in justice to his other children, support me through a four years' course. Besides you know, Mr. Morton, we are four hundred dollars in your debt."

" Should you like very much to go to college, Frank?"

" Better than anything else in the world."

" Then you shall go."

Frank looked up in surprise.

" Don't you understand me?" said Mr. Morton. " I mean that I will defray your expenses through college."

Frank could hardly believe his ears.

" You would spend so much money on me!" he exclaimed, incredulously. " Why it will cost a thousand dollars."

" Very well, I can afford it," said Mr. Morton. " But perhaps you object to the plan."

" How good you are to me," said Frank, impulsively seizing his friend's hand. "What have I done to deserve so much kindness?"

"You have done your duty, Frank, at the sacrifice of your inclinations. I think you ought to be rewarded. God has bestowed upon me more than I need. I think he intends that I shall become his almoner. If you desire to express your gratitude, you can best do it by improving the advantages which will be opened to you."

Frank hastened to his mother to communicate his brilliant prospects. Her joy was scarcely less than his.

"Do not forget, Frank," she said, "who it is that has raised up this friend for you. Give Him the thanks."

There was another whose heart was gladdened when this welcome news reached him in his tent beside the Rappahannock. He felt that while he was doing his duty in the field, God was taking better care of his family than he could have done if he had remained at home.

———

Before closing this chronicle, I must satisfy the curiosity of my readers upon a few points in which they may feel interested.

The Rossville Guards are still in existence, and Frank is still their Captain. They have already done escort duty on several occasions, and once they visited Boston, and marched up State Street with a precision of step which would have done no discredit to veteran soldiers.

Dick Bumstead's reformation proved to be a permanent one. He is Frank's most intimate friend, and with his assistance is laboring to remedy the defects of his early education. He has plenty of ability, and now that he has turned over a new leaf, I have no hesitation in predicting for him a useful and honorable career.

Old Mrs. Payson has left Rossville, much to the delight of her grandson Sam, who never could get along with his grandmother. She still wears for best the "bunnit" presented her by Cynthy Ann, which, notwithstanding its mishap, seems likely to last her to the end of her natural life. She still has a weakness for hot gingerbread and mince pie, and though she is turned of seventy would walk a mile any afternoon, with such an inducement.

Should any of my readers at any time visit the small town of Sparta, and encounter in the street a little old lady dressed in a brown cloak and hood, and firmly grasping in her right hand a faded blue cotton umbrella, they may feel quite certain that they are in the presence of Mrs. Mehitabel Payson, relict of Jeremiah Payson, deceased.

Little Pomp has improved very much both in his studies and his behavior. He now attends school regularly, and is quite as far advanced as most boys

25*

of his age. Though he is not entirely cured of his mischievous propensities, he behaves " pretty well, considering," and is a great deal of company to old Chloe, to whom he reads stories in books lent him by Frank and others. Chloe is amazingly proud of Pomp, whom she regards as a perfect prodigy of talent.

" Lor' bress you, missus," she remarked to Mrs. Frost one day, " he reads jest as fast as I can talk. He's an awful smart boy, dat Pomp."

" Why don't you let him teach you to read, Chloe ? "

" O lor, missus, I could n't learn nohow. I ain't got no gumption. I don't know noffin'."

" Why could n't you learn as well as Pomp ? "

" Dat ar boy's a genus, missus. His fader was a mighty smart nigger, and Pomp's took arter him."

Chloe's conviction of her own inferiority, and Pomp's superior ability seemed so rooted that Mrs. Frost finally gave up her persuasions. Meanwhile, as Chloe is in good health and has abundance of work, she has no difficulty in earning a comfortable subsistence for herself and Pomp. As soon as Pomp is old enough, Frank will employ him upon the farm.

While I am writing these lines intelligence has just been received from Frank's substitute at the seat of war. He has just been promoted to a captaincy. In communicating this he adds : " You may tell

Frank that I am now his equal in rank, though his commission bears an earlier date. I suppose therefore I must content myself with being Captain Frost, Jr. I shall be very glad when the necessities of the country will permit me to lay aside the insignia of rank, and returning to Rossville, subside into plain Henry Frost again. If you ask me when this is to be, I can only say that it depends on the length of our struggle. I AM ENLISTED FOR THE WAR, AND I MEAN TO SEE IT THROUGH! Till that time Frank must content himself with acting as my substitute at home. I am so well pleased with his management of the farm, that I am convinced it is doing as well as if I were at home to superintend it in person. Express to Mr. Waring my gratitude for the generous proposal he has made to Frank. I feel that words are inadequate to express the extent of our obligations to him."

Some years have passed since the above letter was written. The war is happily over, and Captain Frost has returned home with an honorable record of service. Released from duty at home, Frank has exchanged the farm for the college hall; and he is now approaching graduation, one of the foremost scholars in his class. He bids fair to carry out the promise of his boyhood, and in the more varied and prolonged Campaign which manhood opens before him we have reason to believe that he will display equal fidelity and gain an equal success.